# THE SHADOW RIDER

# The Shadow Rider

CHRIS ADAM SMITH

A Black Horse Western

ROBERT HALE · LONDON

© Chris Adam Smith 1997
First published in Great Britain 1997

ISBN 0 7090 5998 1

Robert Hale Limited
Clerkenwell House
Clerkenwell Green
London EC1R 0HT

Photoset in North Wales by
Derek Doyle & Associates, Mold, Flintshire.
Printed and bound in Great Britain by
WBC Book Manufacturers Limited,
Bridgend, Mid-Glamorgan.

This one is for Keith Mason
with fond memories of distant guns
and stillwater trout.

# Author's Note

This is the story of six – sometimes difficult and sometimes pleasurable – months as seen through the eyes of frontier lawman, Wes Harper. His feelings, his thoughts and the bitterness endured at taking the lives of fellow human beings both in war and during the uneasy peace that followed. The wandering federal marshals under state or territorial warrant were tough *hombres*; they had to be, and the majority of them were also men of genuine motive, sincere feeling and capable of great sacrifice. They cared and they made a difference. Life was hard for them and death from the barrel of a smoking sixgun likely and very sudden. They travelled far and wide, paid at the rate of six cents a mile and two dollars for each arrest. An honest federal marshal would have done himself proud to have made $500 in a good year – a poor reward for laying one's life on the line every working day. There is no real end to Marshal Wesley Harper's story, for it is a beginning and the Shadow Rider will come again.

# Prologue

Blackwater Creek, Wyoming Territory, 1873.

The dog kept on barking and yapping and pretty soon the lights in the building were turned down and then out. Chase Hawkins asked Reno George Taverno where the 'breed was and Taverno whispered back that the 'breed was creeping around to the back of the ranch house. Then Hawkins whispered again saying that if he wasn't careful the man would find himself caught in a crossfire. Taverno asked Hawkins did it really matter and Hawkins agreed that, no, it did not really matter at all, what was one 'breed more or less? Then he flicked a blue top with a dirty thumb and read off the time on his plated pocket watch. The flare of the match reflected off the dull nickel silver of the five-pointed deputy's star pinned to his dirty shirt.

Hawkins waited quietly, slowly counting off a hundred to himself. The near full moon popped out briefly from behind a cloud and bathed the ranch house and its dirt yard in a silvery-blue light. He could smell the horses in the small corral off to his left and hear their nervous hard-blown breath

7

as they moved restlessly about the enclosure.

'Twenty-five, twenty-six, twenty-seven....' The dog had stopped its barking and snarling, pacing up and down in front of the long veranda which ran the full length of the darkened, silent building. Walking the length of its rope line pausing, listening before turning to walk back over its previous path. Hawkins watched as a figure, a long gun in its hand, doubled over and, running, made its way across the yard toward the rear of the barn. Billy Tolland getting closer, looking for his two brothers, a family night out.

'Fifty-seven, fifty-eight, fifty-nine....' The horses were fidgeting more noisily now, stamping their restless feet on the hard-packed dirt of the corral. Somewhere far off along Blackwater Creek in among the low growing willow trees there was a splash and a muffled curse and a man afoot stepped off the tangled pathway and into the glistening water. Heck Munroe, the barfly filled with whiskey in order to boost his killing courage. Sammy Ryan was probably with him sharing the bottle. Hawkins guessed that they would need each other's company to lean on in order to get them through the night.

'Seventy-three, seventy-four, seventy-five....' The cold late evening breeze blowing down from the foothills of the Big Horn Mountains and across the open prairie met some resistance from the stand of cottonwoods gathered closely together beyond the cluster of buildings rippling the yellowing leaves, whispering a note of caution to the counting Hawkins.

'Ninety-two, ninety-three, ninety-four....' The creaking windmill took up the song and suddenly began to turn pulling water from deep down in the earth and flushing it out into the near empty, half-sunken corrugated metal tank set into the ground at its base. More muttered curses as a figure stepped clear of the tank, crouched and shifted position away from the cascading water. Wall-eyed Wally Doohan, a man afraid of getting wet on the outside. Nine of them counting the 'breed. That should do it. He quickened the count.

'Ninety-eight, ninety-nine, one hundred.' Hawkins shifted his substantial weight from his left leg to his right, shouldered his lever-action carbine and leaning out from the cover of the barn, shot the dog through the head. His round was echoed by a dozen other guns as men let fly at the building now clearly visible as the last of the thin cloud moved clear of the bright moon illuminating the target almost as if by design.

Lead thudded into the sturdy log walls of the building popping dust and chunks of timber out into the night air. Heavy rifle and pistol bullets smashed the glass windows and ploughed on into the room smashing pottery, china and preserve jars. Bottles disintegrated sending their contents down around the heads of the old couple cowering within. The woman cried out as two rounds splintered wood by her head on their way into the room, buzzing around like angry bees as they ricocheted off the big iron cooking stove.

The old man, an ancient Colt Dragoon gripped in his work-scarred and bony hand, crawled to the woman to comfort her but she was already dead. A large calibre round had penetrated her left temple and smashed its way out behind her right ear. He could see by the moonlight flooding the room that she was beyond earthly help. A lifetime of togetherness ended by a single vicious squeeze of an anonymous trigger-finger. He cradled the woman to him for a moment and then setting her gently on the close-boarded, waxed floor, he wiped tears from his pale eyes, picked up the heavy Colt and crawled to the centre of the floor.

He had to get clear, it was not all going to end for them there; stay alive, wait for the Shadow Rider to come.

Lead was still pouring into the house splintering and smashing at the fabric of the room as he pulled an Indian rug to one side and raised a small trapdoor by its iron ring. Raising it only a foot was opening enough for him to slide his rail-thin body through and down on to the dry and dusty ground beneath the building.

Crawling toward the back of the house the old man could see booted feet running left and right as men moved in for the kill. Added to the light cruelly offered by the bright moon was the flickering glow of burning torches. Long shadows moved swiftly across the yard and men called out, some laughed, some whistled but all sounded delighted with the result of their labours.

Smoke drifted down through the boards above the old man's head and he slid sideways toward the furthest corner. Unseen he emerged from beneath the now burning ranch house and keeping low held to the ever changing patterns of darkness as he made the shelter of the barn. Upright and pressed hard to the wall he circled the tall building and came up to the corral fence. He dodged beneath the rail and catching up one of the terrified horses gamely swung up and on to its back. Holding the animal's mane he kicked it on toward the rail fence.

'Well what do you know,' yelled Hawkins to Reno George Taverno, 'the old Nigger from the woodpile made it out of the fire.' As he spoke he set down his empty carbine, drew his revolver and shot the moving horse out from under the old black man.

Taverno moved quickly to the side of the corral for a clear shot at the downed man but his aim was frustrated by the several ponies milling around close to where the crippled horse was screaming in pain. Two more men rushed to his side, one of them, Santana Vallejo the half-breed, waving a blanket above his head and cursing the rearing horses. He vaulted the rail and moved in closer, suddenly backing off and running back for the fence as the kneeling old man loosed a round from the big Dragoon. The bullet missed the dodging figure but chipped timber away from the rail close by Deputy Chase Hawkins's head sending shards of splintered wood deep into his face and one straight through his left eye. The deputy screamed in agony and dropping his pistol staggered back and away from the corral fence his hands clawing at his injured and bloody face.

The old black man was up and running again. This time he ignored the horses and dived between the rails and made for the stunted willow trees running alongside the creek. A fusillade of lead followed his progress, many of the rounds striking his frail figure. Then, as the roof of the main building ignited there was a rush of fire and flame leaping across the yard to the barn firing the dry

planking with a muffled roar. The gunmen in the
yard suddenly aware of their own peril forgot the
running man and, grabbing the wounded Hawkins, they made for their tethered ponies on the
high ground beyond the inferno, beyond the bitter
smoke and the flames and the flying sparks caught
on the updraft created by the savage fire leaping
from the sun-dried timbers that had once been the
Diamond H headquarters.

# One

Colorado Territory 1874.

The Levi pants did not fit as well as they once had. Close on two years in the Colorado Territorial Prison will do that to a man. Bad food, hard work and stress, combined together in heavy doses, tended to melt the pounds away. I was two years older, twenty-five pounds lighter and my hair had thinned out on my forehead giving me a sharp widow's peak shot with grey. The laughter lines had gone from around my eyes and wide mouth and the tanned skin was close-shaved. But the cracked mirror on the cell wall could not deny my being. The day was mine. The warden had allowed me a bath and a haircut before taking my dirty prison suit away and returning my old clothes, the pants, grey wool shirt and leather vest, and I was feeling the first real unsettling flutter of excitement churning around in my gut. The long denied, deeply hidden dream of ever being free again was surfacing and demanding of me a degree of caution and control, restraints I found difficult to apply.

The bull guard, Mister Danny O'Brian, a huge

red-faced, redheaded Irishman who seemed to have grown into his tight-fitting, blue serge uniform met me at the first gate. He was a kindly man for a prison guard; he played by the rules of the governing regime just as long as the inmates recognized and also played by those same rules. During his periods of duty there were never any beatings, abuse of prisoners or denial of their very basic rights. In my two years of incarceration I had had no trouble with him. He offered me his hand and I shook it firmly.

'This is your day, Harper; you must have mighty powerful friends on the outside.' He smiled, the twinkle in the pale-green eyes added to the richness of his Irish brogue, a broad inflection he had never lost or denied. The man seemed to almost share in my pleasure. 'The old man himself wants to give you the pardon so I would guess that he is counting on the fact that some of those friends have political connections and long memories. Have you said your goodbyes?'

I nodded. 'Yes, thank you, Mister O'Brian.'

There had been no close friends in the two years only grey shoulders to work alongside on the rock pile or within the maintenance gang. Nobody I would miss and no one who would miss me.

I followed him the long length of three, cell-packed corridors from out of which pale and troubled faces watched my passing. Here and there an acquaintance wished me luck and a hand stretched out through the bars. Sometimes there was a curse to go with the goodbye from someone whose trail I had crossed during my two years hard.

A bawdy voice I did not recognize asked me what

was the second thing I was going to do on the outside. A burst of laughter followed the question and then longing mutterings came from darkened souls lying deep within the confines of the iron and steel cages. We passed on by in silence. With each slamming and locking of a door behind me and my continued progress to the last and final slam and rattle before the warden's office door, my heart thumped a little harder. O'Brian led the way in and I followed.

Warden Barstow handed me the pardon document signed and sealed by the territorial governor of Colorado. He passed it to me with a weak handshake and an insincere smile on his thin lips disturbing the neatly trimmed setting of his fledgling moustache. I knew that as soon as the door closed behind me the smile would vanish. I was a free man but Barstow was a prisoner of his own ambitions. He would stay in that miserable place until a political bone was thrown his way and by that time, I guessed, it would be too late for him to enjoy the chewing of it.

The man needed to say something so I waited patiently. You learn a great deal about patience in prison.

'I'm sorry for the mess that brought you here, Harper, and I really am glad that influences on the outside, powerful influences I might add, have made it possible for you to be released without a blemish or stain upon your character.'

I wanted to smile, to yell at him to get on with it but I stood and listened to the speech I guessed he had been rehearsing most of the early morning. I owed the man nothing and yet in some perverse way I was happy for the moment to last knowing that the outcome would be my leaving that stinking hole and his remaining.

'The governor wishes you a safe journey back to Wyoming Territory and there is a travel voucher waiting for you downstairs.' He paused, troubled with the delivery of his next words and I shifted my weight a little with perhaps the beginnings of an irritation I could not suppress. O'Brian coughed and cleared his throat pointedly.

'Just one other point, Harper.' The man's getting there I thought. 'Sheriff Benteen would like you across the county line by sunset. It is a request you understand, not an order. He, Sheriff Benteen, feels there may be those who feel your time was not fully served and may wish you harm. He would rather you were well clear of the county should that happen. The governor has similar feelings about Colorado as a whole....'

His voice trailed off and I turned to O'Brian.

'Can we go, Mister O'Brian?'

O'Brian looked at the warden for confirmation and turning away, led me through the outer door.

O'Brian stayed at my side and walked his measured pace to the property room. A guard slid an envelope across to me which I opened. It contained sixty-two dollars and some loose change, a dog-eared letter from my father, and a photograph of a dark-haired woman with piercing eyes and a smiling full mouth. Not too much to show for my forty-five years of life.

The guard shoved a lumpy gunnysack across to me together with a leather valise. 'Your fancy Colt is in the sack but it's empty and there are no cartridges in the belt. Warden's orders. The rest of your gear including your hat is in the valise. You sign here.' He slid a piece of paper toward me and an inked pen. I didn't sign right away. There should have been more.

'Where will I find my pony?'

'You won't find him at all,' O'Brian answered. 'He took a round when the posse hit you at Indian Wells. Had to be put down. Shame, I hear it was a fine animal.'

'And the saddle, my carbine, the rest of my gear?'

'I believe one of the posse members had it, son. Sold it to help pay off some of the damage you did to their horses. I understand several animals went down as well as yours.'

'I see,' I said softly, suddenly wanting to run at the gate and be gone. The moment passed as the years of moments, panic-filled, long dark moments, had also passed. Controlled and stored away.

O'Brian said, 'You are lucky to have got your fancy pistol back; it has been under lock and key since Benteen brought you in. He wanted it for himself as a matter of fact but your Washington lawyer and colleague insisted it remain on your property list. Perhaps they knew something even back then, eh?'

'Perhaps they did,' I said.

'The swill wagon is about to leave, if you can stand the smell you could ride it into town. I cleared it with the duty man.'

'I think it's a good day for a walk,' I said. 'But thanks anyway, Mister O'Brian.'

I scratched my name on the piece of paper and passed it back over the counter. The guard examined it as though it might be a forgery and then, almost reluctantly, pushed my trappings across to me. I placed the envelope in the leather bag and picked up my returned belongings. O'Brian nodded his head to me and I walked beside him outside and under the high gatehouse roof to the big wood and iron strapped gate. A narrow shaft of sunlight burst in through a man-sized opening and, shaking the bull's big red hand again, I stepped through the gap and into a dusty Colorado morning and a freedom of sorts.

Strange how the thickness of a prison door can so distort the weather. From the drab grey morning of the prison yard and out into the bright clear morning sunshine was like stepping into another world. Inside I had not noticed just how blue the sky was or the fact that it was littered with small birds darting and diving over the long late-summer grass which grew in abundance just a hundred yards or so beyond the prison walls. The driver of the pig-swill wagon raised his hand to me but I waved him away and watched as the creaking wagon made for the distant township shimmering in a hazy puddle, floating feet above the horizon. As the wagon cleared on past I could see beyond it a rider and two horses moving in at a fast canter toward the prison. A big man wearing a tall black hat, clothes protected from the trail dust by a long, flowing canvas coat. I could hear the measured thud of the horses' hooves as they hit the sunbaked dirt road and somehow I knew he was coming for me.

I waited for maybe four or five minutes and as he drew closer so the swill wagon with its stinking load grew fainter and with it the stench. I could still smell the prison but that odour was ingrained in me. It had impregnated my clothes, soaked into the pores of my skin and into my hair and it would take many weeks of bathing and laundering to rid me of that peculiar fragrance, a combination of close confinement and fear. I also knew from experience that sometimes, on certain people, the odour never completely dissipated. It faded with time but nevertheless was always there. It was a smell, a spoor I had for many years followed. The awareness of that stink, had, in part, been my stock in trade.

I pulled my crumpled Stetson out of the valise and stood there in the sunshine.

The oncoming rider turned off the trail 200 yards out and cut through the long grass toward the main prison gate. Clearing the grass he slowed the animals to a walk and brought them to a dusty halt in front of me.

'Hi, Wes, sorry I'm late.'

'Hello Jack. You're not late, I wasn't waiting for you. Did not expect you,' I said coldly.

'That really true, Wes?' he asked.

United States Marshal Jack Brubaker out of Denver City had a deep nut-brown voice, brown eyes and a richly dark-tanned skin. He was an outdoors man. A big man, six foot two inches and weighing a hefty 200 pounds and very little of that given to fat. He was five years older than me, three inches taller and around sixty pounds heavier. He wiped the dust from his drooping moustache with a red bandanna and looked down at me. He had once been and I supposed still was, my best friend.

'Yes, it's true, Jack. I didn't expect to see you today, tomorrow, not ever.'

'Who do you think worked so hard to get you

your Goddammed pardon? To get your butt out of that hell-hole?' he asked pulling up the head of the tall horse fidgeting restlessly between his knees.

'You did that, Jack, but then you put me in there in the first place.'

'It was the law put you in there, Wes. The law you worked for.'

'That was not my law, that was your law, Jack.' I did not feel like debating the finer points of the law standing in the hot sun outside of the territorial prison. Also my neck ached from looking up at him. He seemed even taller than I remembered. I was aware that the guards were watching us from the tower and the built-up elation I had suppressed all of the morning and the long night before was becoming unglued.

'You sure are a sorry-looking son-of-a-bitch, Wes, standing there with your wherewithals and nowhere to go. Now, are you getting up on that damned horse or what? I've rented these nags by the hour out of my own money and I'm a poor man.'

I sighed and suddenly felt very tired. Picking up my bags I walked over to the spare saddlehorse and hung them over the saddle horn. I raised the fender and checked the cinch-strap, it was tight and the stirrup leather seemed about the right length. The saddle creaked as I swung aboard and settled my backside into the hard polished seat.

'Nice horse, Jack.' I said, meaning it.

'Only the best for you, Wes; don't fall off. You got a coat?'

'No, keep out of the dust. We'll ride across the grassland I want to smell it. God how I want to smell it.'

'Yes, I bet you do, old friend,' was all he said.

# TWO

Jack Brubaker and me went way back. Way back to the time when before the Civil War we were both deputies working out of Fort Morgan. I had just joined the US Marshals Service while Brubaker had been wearing the badge for five years. He was an old-timer even then. Not in years but in experience. There was something that set him apart from other lawmen. He was a gentleman but tough and hellish fast with an iron. Looking at him there riding ahead of me, a big man on a big horse, an old friend, it was hard to remember that he had brought me in to Denver to a trial that should never have been.

I am no great horseman and if there is a railroad or a stageline I will take it everytime out of preference to a long day sitting a cold, often wet leather saddle. If there is a trail I'll buggy it but if needs must, and they often do in these vast territories, I can ride hard with the best of them. Like then, letting Brubaker push on out in front while I got my wind and then kicking the animal on to ride on by him and set the beast at a dead run through the dark green grass, my hat slipping to the back of my head held there by the braided thong, while the pony settled to its own pace and I embraced the wind and the sweet scent of crushed herbs and swaying wildflowers.

I slowed the animal, brought him in with my knees, neck reined him to the left and slowed him down fearful that my trappings were going to spill from the bag and spread themselves out all over the prairie. We sat there in the sun blowing the animals and ourselves, sweat running down our backs laughing. Then sipping warm whiskey from Brubaker's hip flask and laughing some more, the blue sky above us, the territorial prison far behind.

'Where'd you get the horses?' I asked.

'Pacerville; I thought we'd give Canon City a miss. It's a ride but hell we got all day.'

He was right but the way we pushed those horses it did not take us all day to get there.

Pacerville was very much the same as any other small railhead cowtown running up from Fort Worth and on to Denver and Cheyenne. One dusty, dirty and tired main street beginning with stockyards and ending with a livery stable and very little else in between.

We dropped the tired horses off at the livery and Brubaker tipped the boy a dollar on his promise to rub them down, water and grain them. The kid had probably never earned a whole dollar that way in his life and his wide-eyed and willing gap-toothed smile assured my companion that his wishes would be met to the letter.

Brubaker had timed it well. As we walked along Pacerville's main street he told me the Union Pacific locomotive would arrive just short of three o'clock which gave us time for one cold beer each at the dilapidated and near-empty saloon. We drank our frothy beers in silence. I suppose, all things considered, happy in one another's company.

He had been right of course. He had not had any choice but to take me in and, in doing so, he probably saved my life. Benteen and his posse didn't want to take a prisoner. Also, there was no doubt in my mind that he had been more than instrumental in obtaining my pardon. Still, I had been telling the truth when I had told him I was surprised to see him. He had a big reputation to protect and any political ambitions he may have harboured would not be enhanced in any way by meeting a discredited lawman, even a pardoned one, fresh from the territorial prison. Maybe, when I was quieter inside I would talk to him, tell him of my feelings. Make him aware of what prison is like for an ex-lawman. I owed as much in some ways to Danny O'Brian as I did to Brubaker. The old bull had kept me alive and out of harm's way on more than one occasion. That was another debt and one which some day I aimed to repay in spades.

We left the saloon walking side by side to the depot. Brubaker stopped briefly at the hotel to pay his overnight bill and to pick up his gear and I bought two boxes of .45 shells from the general store, there not being a resident gunsmith in Pacerville.

A dark-suited, black-bearded fat man was leaning on one of the porch uprights. He watched as we came on, then ignoring me he spoke directly to Brubaker.

'Hello, Marshal, surprised to see you down this way.'

'Hi there, George, how have you been? Thought they had you voted out at the last election,' said

Brubaker with an easy smile on his forlorn-looking face.

'You don't care too much who you travel with do you, Jack?'

It was not a question so Brubaker ignored it, sitting himself down on the long wooden bench and pulling a Denver newspaper from the pocket of his black frock coat. But I did not ignore it, I could not. I had spent the last two long years of my life watching my language, taking care, being polite to snot-nosed prison guards who could have made my life hell and short when O'Brian wasn't around if I had given them cause.

'I got your message, Benteen, there was no need for you to check it out.'

'I knew you'd get it sure enough, Harper, I just wanted to be sure you left my county.'

George Benteen had been the county sheriff for too long. He neither had liking nor respect for the electorate but they kept on voting him into office anyway because he was good at his job. Not in the sense that Brubaker was a fine peace officer but in the sense that he kept the county pretty much free of trouble by ensuring that his deputies kept an often itinerant workforce fairly well subjugated. A pistol whipping in a dark alley or a bullet for a suspected thief was as good a deal on justice as one could expect from George Benteen.

'I got a full pardon, Benteen. I'm no business of yours; I'm leaving the county because I choose to leave it not because you think you can haze me like some two-bit drunken cowboy.' My voice was angry, I felt angry but in control.

'A pardon don't make you smell good, it just means some folks pulled some legal strings to get you out is all,' said Benteen bitterly.

'Not true,' I countered, almost wanting the argument. 'The pardon leaves me clean and clear.'

'You killed the Lattimer boys as sure as you are standing there, Harper, and you used your Goddamned federal badge to do it.'

'They came for me, George, came right at me is the way it was and you knew that right enough but chose to ignore it.'

'Well it isn't over, Harper; Bob Lattimer and Charlie Wilcox know you're out and they want a piece of you that's why I want you out of my county.'

'You have knowledge of the planning of a malicious assault and have ignored it?' asked Brubaker quietly, looking up from his newspaper. 'Why, George, that almost makes you an accomplice after the fact.'

Benteen spat tobacco juice near to my boot and glared at Brubaker. 'It's not a federal offence, Brubaker, and I've warned him about it coming his way. Was I you I wouldn't stand too close to him for a while. Apart from the stink of prison rubbing off on you, you are liable to take a round yourself you stand too close to Wesley Harper.'

I stepped forward then and hit the man in the face. In the mouth with my left fist and on the nose with my right, breaking it at the bridge. He staggered back and I hit him again on his gushing nose. His scream was drowned by the locomotive's whistle as the Denver-bound train snorted its way around the corner and hissed to a stop. I waited to see if Benteen would try to get to his feet but he did not; he just sat there glaring at me through the tears misting his hate-filled eyes. I have rarely seen a man offer so much unspoken hatred. There was blood mixed with tobacco spittle all down the front of his white shirt and fancy silk vest.

Brubaker picked up my bags and ignoring the fallen sheriff stepped up on to the train. I followed him wishing that it had not happened that way.

# THREE

About a half-day's easy-paced ride to the south-
west of Denver City to where Cherry Creek divides
into two, the main creek rolling down toward the
South Platte and the run-off stream spins its
cheerful way through rich timberland before it too
splashes into the river, Jack Brubaker maintains a
small hunting cabin. It is out of the way and hidden
deep in untrailed country. One day after our
arrival in Denver and after reporting briefly into
his office, Brubaker hired us two good saddle
ponies and we left for that cabin.

The cabin was remote, off the beaten track and
likely only to be discovered by a wandering Indian
who would avoid contact with the inhabitants or a
like-minded hunter who needed shelter and
respected another hunter's property. After all, line
shacks running at long intervals across endless
ranch boundaries and as often as not unmanned
were never in any way vandalized other than by
rodents or the odd inquisitive bear.

The large fireplace and the iron cooking stove
were well stocked with cut cordwood and the larder
packed with canned goods. Brubaker was only a
passing fair country cook but he could make very

drinkable coffee.

Summer was almost at an end and although the midday sun burned down through the clear air the leaves on the trees were already beginning to turn. Walking through the woods with Brubaker's double twelve gauge under my arm on the evening of the second day following my release from prison it was hard for me to accept the reality of my situation. At one point I had to sit down close by the low running creek in order to stop the trembling of my legs, the wild beating of my heart and the tears which threatened at any moment to flood my eyes. I dipped my hand in the clear water and splashed it across my face glad that I was alone.

Walking back toward the cabin I could still smell the damp creek on the mist swirling in from the willows and taste the brewing coffee drifting out to meet me mixed in and overtaken by the sweet scent of the woodsmoke from the cooking stove. The horses called me as I passed by the small corral and I answered them with quiet words.

'Didn't hear you fire that thing,' said Brubaker as I entered the cabin and hung the scattergun from a peg beside the door.

'Nothing much about, Jack, too early in the day I guess.'

'You are a dumb liar, Wes, the woods are alive with game at this time of the year. It's been a good summer for them. But, man, I think I know how you feel about freedom and the silence and we can go without fresh meat for a day or two or whenever.' He grinned at me and I realized then and there something of the very special nature of Jack Brubaker.

'Coffee smells good,' I said, hoping to hide some

of the foolishness I felt at not being able to cap a rabbit.

'How's some fish sound to you?'

'Sounds fine, Jack.'

'You're damned right it does. About three-quarters of a mile along the creek there is a deep hole and some fat trout hiding therein. I promise you I got a fly they cannot resist.'

Even stripped of his black suit and kitted out in work-worn and faded range clothes there was something very authoritative about Jack Brubaker. Watching him cracking eggs into a skillet with a striped apron around his waist and biscuit flour in his drooping moustache he still looked like a man to be taken seriously.

I thought of the smart and fancy-vested George Benteen and his interpretation of the law compared to Jack Brubaker's and it was difficult to believe they served the same legal system. Of course, in many ways they did not. Federal officers such as Brubaker, or myself when I had packed a badge, serve very different jurisdictions. Benteen was restricted to his county boundary whereas we roamed free on federal business chasing fugitives from Chicago to Nogalas, mail thieves from San Franscisco to Lafayette. It gave the man with the federal warrant a wider perspective of the law in one way but a tighter one in another. Take away the pure politics of elected sheriffs and you had a law that really counted for something. Although not entirely free of political influence, a US marshal is a Washington appointment, federal law somehow seemed more pure although at times greatly resented by the free-spirited cowboys and ranchers it often ensnared. Yet in its purest form it was the reason Jack Brubaker took me to Denver and got me tried and convicted and then struggled uphill for two years to get that verdict overturned.

After supper I dumped out the contents of my gunnysack on to the rough, polished pine table. It contained the essential tools of my trade. Were I a carpenter it would have been a hammer, a chisel, a rasp or a fine plane. If a doctor, then a scalpel, liniments a stethoscope, bandages and ether. But I had been a lawman, a deputy US marshal and the main tools of my trade were my sixgun and its accoutrements.

The holster had been fashioned from a single piece of oiled black leather. There was a dull bloom to parts of the hide where it had dried out over the two years of neglect. I oiled it together with the shellbelt and filled the thirty-six loops with grey-nosed, brass-cased shells. Brubaker sat down to watch asking my permission before picking up the big revolver. It was a single action .45 Colt Peacemaker with a five and a half inch barrel. The gun was heavily silver-plated and scroll engraved by hand at the Colt factory in Hartford, Connecticut. The grips were made of carved ivory showing an eagle with half-folded wings grasping a Union flag in its chiselled talons. It was a very special, very expensive, one-off, pre mass-production piece, manufactured many months before the .45 Colt became the standard issue sidearm of the US military.

There was a brief sentiment engraved on the backstrap: *Wesley Harper – For all my tomorrows. 1872.*

Brubaker hefted the piece, cocked it and testing the sear, squeezed the trigger setting the hammer down under restraint from his thumb.

'Anyone else other than me know who gave you this?' Brubaker asked.

'No, no one at all that I am aware of.'

'You could have made a lot out of it.'

'It would not have been right to do it that way.'

'Maybe not, but he called in a lot of favours to help get that pardon without showing too much of his hand. It raised a few Goddamned eyebrows in Washington.'

'And there was me thinking that you did it all by yourself, Jack,' I grinned at the big man.

'Did you know Benteen wanted it? Got his hands on it once. Tried to steal it when I took you from the posse out at Indian Wells. Jesus Christ that was a mess. Dead horses everywhere. Three men wounded, two dead Lattimers, and you barely semi-conscious and Benteen about to cap a round between your eyes.'

'It was one hell of a mess, Jack, but you got to the truth of it else I wouldn't be here now. And yes, I did know about Benteen wanting the Colt. The bull at the prison told me about it.'

'You were set up good but you went in without a federal warrant.'

'The Lattimers were as guilty as hell and had it not been for Benteen's interference I maybe could have brought them in alive. They were all strung out, damn it.'

'It was Benteen's bailiwick and he's never had any time for federal law.'

'George and Billy Lattimer were cold-blooded killers, Jack; they took down the Denver stage, killed the guard, crippled the driver, took the mailbags and Benteen knew it. Could be little brother Bobby and Charlie Wilcox were in on it with them. I gave them every chance to surrender and maybe they would have if Benteen and his rowdies had not busted in there.

'It's water under the bridge, Wes.' His voice was kindly, gentle, counterpointing my own loud, angry words.

'Maybe so but it will never run clear enough for me.' I meant that but the anger that had preceded the words was spent. I shrugged, suddenly weary of it all.

'You were one sure enough marshal,' said Brubaker sensing my shifting mood and deftly changing the subject. 'Until Indian Wells, Washington thought you would go far, my friend, maybe even US Marshal of the Territory. Wyoming that is,' he added with a dry chuckle. 'You know what they used to call you in the Nations?'

'No.'

'The Shadow Rider.'

'Shadow Rider?' I asked, curious, having never heard the term before.

'Yeah, the Shadow Rider, on account of you were there before anyone saw you coming and you always came in the evening, in the long shadows. You and that big bay.'

'Uhm,' was all I could think of to say.

'You had that bay a good many years, Wes.'

'Horse, I called him Horse.' I remembered him then sadly, and it must have showed.

'If it helps any, Wes, it was me put him down.'

'Thanks,' I said absently, lost in my thoughts of what seemed a long time ago, the Lattimers forgotten, my uniform freshly pressed, my duty clear.

*The men came out of the twilight at us and we were*

*somewhere on that summer's evening we should not have been. I could smell the roses and the perfume and the liquor and hear the laughter coming from within the large, boldly-lit, white, long-galleried house. There were three of us on duty that evening guarding the life of a man who should have been miles away in Washington dealing with matters that were, in their way, important to us all. But he was not there, he was in a perfumed house in Maryland on the shores of Chesapeake Bay relaxing from the rigours of the ever growing daily burden heaped upon his chunky shoulders. Like all men he had his weaknesses and that house the whiskey and fine cigars that went with it were three of them. The post changed at eight o'clock and as I came on duty and returned a private's crisp salute, the man stepped out on to the veranda to join me. An aide fired his cigar for him and he walked over to my side. I believe he was about to speak to me, to share a moment with a man who was, apart from the sleeping hours, constantly at his side. As he removed the cigar from his mouth the two men stepped out from behind the rose bushes. How they had infiltrated our perimeter I was never able to discover and, at that particular moment in time it mattered little to me. One man raised a shotgun and the other a pistol. I stepped round in front of my charge and took the first pistol round in the side just above my polished leather holster and sword belt, the second I took in the upper left arm. I shot the man armed with the 12 gauge through the left eye and dropped his companion with three rounds in the chest before I fell away and down the polished steps and on to the sweet-smelling, freshly mown grass. I believed myself to be dying and was afraid, and yet in some curious way, satisfied that I had died fulfilling the task entrusted to me. He came to see me in the Armory Square Hospital in Washington; he came to see a lot of young men that day. He gave out medals and*

*words of comfort. Later he found me in the garden sitting*
*in the afternoon sunshine watching the daisies grow and*
*happy to be alive. He did not give me a medal but he*
*presented me with the cased Colt revolver and a promise.*
*He told me that he would watch my career with interest,*
*remember me with fondness and should I ever need his*
*help and it was within his power to give it, then I only had*
*to ask. I remembered thinking that I liked him very much*
*and that he was a short man for such a tall job.*

I stripped the Colt, oiled it and reassembled it. I
stood up and swung the black shellbelt around my
waist and slid the holster around to my left hip with
the ivory butt almost to my navel. The belt was a
little loose and Brubaker dug out a hole-punch and
I worked another inch out of the silver mounted
buckle. It sat right and felt snug.

I stood there feeling a little foolish but tried the
draw nevertheless. It was fast enough and with a
little practice would speed up some, give me an
edge if I needed it. I reholstered the weapon.

'Haven't you forgotten something?' Brubaker
asked.

'Yeah,' I said, taking it out again and loading it.

We drank whiskey and water long into the night
and until long after the log fire had faded.

That night I dreamed of screaming horses and
pistol fire in the half light. Twisting and turning away
from the gunfire and tangling my blankets into knots
I saw the Lattimers riding hard at me and felt the
silver Colt filling my hand. Seconds later I saw them
falling away among flailing hooves, Billy Lattimer
the younger of the two brothers, struggling to his feet
and falling away again as the big Colt rolled in my
hand. Then Benteen and his deputies yelling,

coming in behind the fallen men, Horse jerking hard beneath me, going down, but still running at the guns as I fell from the saddle. More gunfire, some from my own hand and some from the growing darkness. My eyes were filled with blood from an unremembered blow and Benteen was leering down at me a rifle in his hand. Then Jack Brubaker yelling for him to drop the weapon and the gun coming up to me and firing anyway. I got out of the narrow bed hot and terrified within myself that if I went back to sleep the round from Benteen's rifle would pass through me instead of by my ear as it had, the weapon deflected by a blow from the big US marshal. I listened to Brubaker snoring in the one separate bedroom and taking the makings from his vest pocket I rolled a thin cigarette. I am not a heavy smoker but sometimes it helps. Sitting with a blanket around my shoulders I waited for the first glow of sunrise afraid to return to my bed.

We fished the creek together over the next few weeks and both caught our fair share of trout. We ate them grilled, pan-fried, cold and barbecued. We ate trout until Brubaker could stand it no longer and he set aside my desire for the continued silence and took the scattergun out to the woods and brought back with him a brace of cottontails for our supper.

Earlier I had heard the weapon discharge, both barrels sounding almost as one and knew then that the sojourn was nearly over.

'I have to ride into Denver tomorrow for a few days but I will be back here by Friday. You can come with me or you can stay here,' said Brubaker, as I sat back in my chair rocking it on to its back legs and picking rabbit from between my teeth with a shaved matchstick.

'I'll wait here for you, Jack, but I think come Sunday I'll be riding on. Maybe go home and see how old Moke is getting on.'

'You heard from the old fart?'

'Not since Dad passed away. He kind of left the place in Moke's care and I'm happy with that.'

'Tough, your old man dying like that while you were inside.'

'It would have been tough wherever I was. Wherever I was, I was never at home. That was the job, I guess.'

'I can maybe get your badge back for you, given a couple of months. You could ride out of the Denver office again for me.'

'You think they'd let me?'

'You have powerful friends, Wes.'

I handed him a letter I had written the night before to the Cattleman's Bank in Denver City asking that my account be closed and the money given to Brubaker.

'There's about seven hundred dollars in the account, Jack, I'd like you to buy me a .45 Colt Army with a seven and a half inch barrel and a shellbelt and holster to go with it. Black or brown hide, the colour doesn't matter. I'll store this pistol for a while; it kind of stands out in a crowd if you know what I mean. Also get me a Winchester carbine in .44-40 and a box of shells. I like the big bay we hired, maybe Stobley, the livery manager, will sell him with the rig. Ask him, will you please, and get a bill of sale if he trades fair.'

'And if he doesn't?'

'Then I'll steal it, what the hell?'

'You got a plan for the future, Wes?' he asked me, his voice, I thought, a little concerned.

'I think I'll ride up beyond the Deer Creek Range country, call in on old Moke and chew the fat, see if he's OK and then maybe ride up into Idaho for a spell, come back this way in the spring and see how it goes, take you up on the offer of a job if the offer still holds good.'

'It's hard winter country up there in the mountains.'

'It's going to be hard winter country all over for me for a long while yet, Jack. I'll see it through.'

# FOUR

Brubaker left for Denver early the following morning. I rolled out of my bunk and shared a pot of scalding black coffee with him and together we watched as the first early glow of morning splashed along a distant horizon and filtered its misty way in through the surrounding woodland. He made a string of somewhat derogatory jokes about my appearance, sitting there at the table in my red drawers and dusty boots, shirtless but with the crumpled grey Stetson hat sitting low on the front of my head. I told him I was trying to air out the smell of the prison and he reassured me that it had long since gone. We talked for a while about how the mark stayed with some men forever and shared a few names of past hard men, hunted and usually captured fugitives, and then he was gone, riding the big horse out through the open yard, into the trees vanishing from my view within seconds.

I had my day planned out and after another pot of coffee I set to scrubbing out my clothes not entirely convinced by Brubaker's kind words. I filled the wooden bucket with Levis, drawers, shirt and socks and boiled a giant kettle of ice-cold well-water on the iron cooking stove. I turned the valise upside down and shook it out for anything I might have missed. The envelope fell on to the table and settled there waiting for me to pick it up. Almost daring me to do it. I was almost afraid to touch it let alone open it in the privacy of the cabin. In the prison storeroom with O'Brian and the guard clerk watching my every move it had been a simple thing to glance at the photograph and push it back into the darkness.

The sepia-toned picture fell easily into my open hand. Theresa Meyer. Dark short hair, gentle full mouth, green eyes above high cheek bones. Laughter lines lurking around her mouth, the camera frozen sparkle of her smile. A smile to be kissed as we rolled through the world together.

Theresa Meyer and her seven-year-old son, Jonah. The woman desperately trying to find a settled future for the both of them and the young boy on his own quest, trying to make sense of enjoying the company of a man who was not his father but who loved his mother. Seeming to come to terms with the fact that he liked seeing the man and his mother together.

Jonah's father had died bravely, the War Department had written her telling her that. Theresa had told me about it, the man fighting under General Joe Hooker's command. He had fallen with honour at Marye's Heights overlooking the Rapphannock River in Virginia on a cold December morning way back in 1862. A lot of brave young men had died with honour on that bloody battlefield east of Fredricksburg. 9000 men fell under the Rebel guns. Brave men running, many shot in the back by musket fire or blown to pieces by exploding canister while turning away

from an impenetrable blast of Southern firepower.
I had been one of them, turned at a grey stone wall
by the sharpshooters of the 24th Georgia and
running back like a frightened buck. Maybe I had
even shoved Jonah's father out of the way in the
panic, trodden on his body or overtaken him
before the Minié ball or jagged shrapnel or
whatever other method his way of passing over had
been. But I had never told either Theresa or the
boy of those things.

I wondered what Theresa was doing then, at that
very moment. Jonah asleep still, he was a hard boy
to rouse in the mornings. And she? Lying beside
Aaron Shiffner, warm, comfortable and safe in the
knowledge that he would be there for her each and
every night. At six in the evening for supper and at
six in the morning for breakfast. For the summer
dance and for church each Sunday. Maybe by now
they had other children, perhaps Jonah had a sister
or a brother, maybe both. I stared at those lips
trying to remember what her last words to me had
been and remembering there had been no last
words. Hot tears and wet lips and a naked
demanding body pressed against me. Not words
but feelings, sensations I would never forget.

I thought of that soulful prison voice, asking,
what would be the second thing I would do.
Thinking of his needs and mine and how very
different each man's needs are, have to be in order
for the very fabric of the world to survive in any
decent order. Of how a man grew up, even an
older man, and found a greater maturity with love.
A month, a week, even a day before I had met
Theresa I could have answered that man in prison,
sympathized with his question, shared his desire.

But something in the handsome woman had changed me. I shrugged it off, that had been a long time ago and although my feelings toward women in general had become somewhat ambivalent my desire for her had never in any way diminished.

Theresa's father was the town doctor, an influential man. A softly spoken individual who wanted some sort of real peace for his only child and his young grandson. He counselled her against me, my way of life and his argument had prevailed. I could give up the badge and have her or it would be best that I ride on. I had chosen Theresa, there was simply no other choice to make. However, I had had one last duty to perform and it was agreed I clear the books with the service before handing in my shield.

On the face of it a simple enough, routine assignment. I had to escort a fugitive from the Denver marshals' office down to Amarillo in the Texas Panhandle. A six-week round trip at most which ended up taking a long and bitter full year. Either because I was too relaxed or because he was extra smart, my prisoner, a gunfighter named Arkansas Bob Deacon, escaped. I trailed him down through Kansas, across the border and into Missouri and then further south and into his home state. I lost him somewhere in the Arkansas River country when he doubled back into Northern Texas, our original destination. I picked up his trail again and with the aid of a Texas Ranger patrol I rearrested him and the small gang he had gathered together with him. We delivered him to the overnight keeping of a deputy sheriff in Adobe Bend. He bribed the officer and escaped again, only that time he shot and wounded one of the rangers before shooting me through both thighs. A heavy calibre round entered my left thigh just below my pistol holster and burned its way through both legs before exiting through my right leg three inches above the knee.

Although there is still an outstanding warrant on Bob Deacon he has never to my knowledge been retaken.

When I had finally returned home to Blackwater, Theresa was promised to Aaron Shiffner the county attorney and my cause was lost. Young Jonah's future took precedence over matters of the heart. We spent three short idyllic hours together at the line-camp on my father's property before she left me with a long kiss and a bittersweet memory. I could still taste that kiss even then, sitting there alone in Jack Brubaker's cabin four years on.

I reassigned to Washington as part of the presidential team of US marshals on bodyguard duty. Since that day I have never been home to Blackwater Creek or to my father's ranch, the Diamond H, and I was not sure that I was ready for that even now.

I scrubbed my clothes and rinsed them in clean fresh water, and still dressed as I had been at breakfast, I set out with my wooden bucket full of clean laundry towards the corral fence where I had strung a drying line from the highest rail to a rusty iron peg driven hard into the privy wall. I was halfway across the yard when I noticed the silence, the stillness of a birdless sky. Usually at that early time of the day small birds would be chirping out a chorus of territorial and feeding calls as they flitted their way from tree to tree storing up the fat before the hidden winter, slowly revealing itself in the golden leaves and the cold mornings, finally lurched into view.

The lessons I had learned over the long years of being a peace officer had not deserted me during my two years hard time. If the woods were too quiet then there had to be a reason for it. An Indian maybe? I had seen one fishing further along the creek but he gathered up his gear and left before I could approach him. A bear? Not so likely, they would have moved to higher ground by now seeking winter shelter. It had to be a man, or men.

I casually set the bucket down in the yard and turning slowly, I began to walk back toward the house. I had gone only a few steps when something buzzed past my ear and thudded into the woodwork of the cabin. The buzzing was immediately followed by the crack of a pistol and I doubled over and dodged from left to right as I covered the ground between myself and the open cabin door. Three more hornets sang past me and slapped into the door-frame as I cleared the porch and, diving forward, rolled into the semi-gloom of the cabin, then sideways behind the open door's protective cover. I was sweating like a hard-run horse.

No more fire came into the cabin so, after several minutes, I slid crabwise across the floor and reaching up grasped the smooth stock of the shotgun pulling it down on to the floor beside me. Again reaching up and feeling along the shelf I tipped over the cartridge box bringing down a stream of orange-coloured shells about my ears. Sitting up with my back to the thick lower outside wall I broke open the gun, dropped two rounds into the breach and quietly closed it. I pulled the hammers on to full-cock and moving quietly crawled toward the doorway where I could see out on to the yard through the crack of the door's wide jamb. I watched as Bobby Lattimer slid from behind the corral and withdrew from my line of fire behind the privy.

I sat back down on the floor and waited. It was his play or maybe it was Charlie Wilcox calling the shots this morning. There was paper on him from way back although, as far as I knew, young Lattimer's name was not yet on any federal warrant.

'Best you come on out here, old man, we got you bang to rights and we'll burn you out if'n we have to.' A young voice from behind the privy.

So Bobby wanted to talk.

'You were smart, Bobby, you'd get your ass out of here. No harm done yet. I'm scared but I'm not hurt and I still carry a federal badge.' I called it out softly across the yard.

'He don't got no federal badge, Bobby, he's shittin' you.' That was George Benteen whispering somewhere behind Lattimer and the privy. Some way off, still out in the woods.

'You ain't got no badge to hide behind, Harper, I know that much,' Lattimer called back.

'Benteen's a fool, Bobby, he knows from nothing; you follow that man you will follow him to Hell.' I could still sound tough and colourful with it.

They wouldn't have ridden all this way with Benteen and not have a plan. They must have scouted the cabin before making their move.

Charlie Wilcox was probably trying to blindside me by coming up at the cabin from the rear where there were no windows. I guessed Lattimer had been ordered to keep me talking awhile.

'Bobby, your brothers were no damned good and I took them out. The law backed my hand eventually so you have no call to fight with me.' As I talked I crawled toward the rear of the cabin getting to my feet when I was certain his line of sight from the privy was obscured by the half-open door.

Jack Brubaker was a US marshal of long standing. He was a wily old fox and no way would he have built himself a cabin with one blind side. Too many guns could be out there waiting for him. Every once in a while a badman wants revenge and will make a try for the badge that brought him down. A lawman lives with that thought. Or sometimes he dies without it. A third of the way along the wall, about shoulder height, just above where the cabin's construction changed from logs to the sawn lumber of the upper third, Brubaker had cut a small port. It was about six inches wide and four inches high. The hole was covered by an oblong of matching lumber held in place by a nail and part of a leather belt. I released the leather from the nail and slowly lowered the flap. Charlie Wilcox was treading carefully through the undergrowth, strain showing on his bearded face, a cocked pistol held forward in each hand. I needed another ten yards before I could use the shotgun and I toyed with the idea of crossing the room to my bunk and getting the Colt but decided against it.

'What's it going to be, Harper, you coming out or

what?' Lattimer called, irritation and nervousness edging his thin voice, raising its pitch.

'Or what, Bobby?' I shouted over my shoulder measuring each step that Wilcox took, each yard of ground he covered. The man paused and for a moment I wondered if he had noticed a change in the sound of my voice now that the little flap was open. But that was not the reason for him stopping. He shoved one pistol under his left arm and pulled a filthy handkerchief from the pocket of his long overcoat, wiped his wet face and shoved the rag back out of sight. I waited patiently as he moved forward again.

'You got two minutes, Harper, then we're going to burn that shack down around your Goddamned ears,' Lattimer yelled.

I held the twin tubes of the twelve gauge an inch from the opening and told Wilcox, 'Drop them pistols, Charlie, or I'll cut you in half.'

He turned, puzzled, still not spotting the hole in the wall, the pistols coming up as I pulled both triggers of the shotgun. The heavy blast took him squarely in the chest tossing him backwards, the front of his long coat peppered with shot, dust and disintegrated wool. He fired neither pistol but lay down heavily on his back in the thick undergrowth his feet kicking down hard, the silver-rowelled Mexican spurs scratching deep grooves in the soft ground.

My ears were ringing. In the confusion of the moment I had forgotten to protect them and I could barely hear Bobby Lattimer shouting from behind the privy, frightened, almost screaming, asking Charlie Wilcox if he had shot me dead.

'No, Bobby,' I called back, 'as a matter of fact it

didn't quite go down that way for friend Charlie.' As I called to him I broke the shotgun and pulling out the smoking hulls I slipped two fresh ones into the breach and snapped it closed. Through the door jamb I could see Lattimer backing away from the privy the pistol held high, pointing more toward the sky than at me. I also heard the crash of a horse and rider breaking through the brush behind him and the fading sound of a pony's hooves. Bobby Lattimer heard it as well.

I stepped clear of the door, standing there in my long john's telling the young desperado to drop the piece knowing he would not do it and pulling the front trigger of the scattergun as Bobby's pistol came level, watching as the shot exploded dust from the front of his canvas jacket sending him backwards into the darkness from which, I supposed, he had once come.

Bobby Lattimer was very dead. No question about it. The shot from the full-choked barrel had taken him in the chest and neck at optimum range. I walked back to the cabin scrubbing at my ears hoping to lessen the ringing but I knew from past experience that it would be several days before the drums settled down again. I washed my hands in the sink's tin bowl and pulled on some pants and a shirt before returning to the interrupted chore of hanging my clothes on to the makeshift line. The birds were singing again, fluttering about in the trees, going about their daily business of staying alive, and a fresh breeze had drifted the smoke and sour smell of the blackpowder cartridges away from the cabin and the yard.

It took me nearly two hours to dig a grave in the

soft soil close by the creek. I decided it was easier and probably quite fitting that the two men should share the one grave so I dug it a little wide to accomodate the pair of them.

Dragging Lattimer on to a tarpaulin I had found in the cabin's storeroom was easy; he was a lightweight and, I guessed, not much more than eighteen, nineteen years old. I dragged the canvas to the graveside and rolled him off and into it, surprised that he landed in the bottom with a splash, suddenly realizing that the hole was filling with water from the boggy ground surrounding it. I did not think it would matter too much to either of the men.

Charlie was heavier and I played with the thought of getting a rope on him and letting the bay take the strain but decided against the idea. It took a while and a stop or two but I finally rolled Charlie Wilcox in on top of the completely immersed Bobby Lattimer and tossed the bloody tarp in on top of the both of them. Filling in the hole was a lot easier than digging it out had been.

Finding something to say over the two men was difficult. I thought about it and got to wondering what they would have said over me had it gone down the other way. They probably would not have bothered to bury me at all.

The sun was high in the sky arching its long way out to the west when I cleaned the shovel in the creek and made my way back to Brubaker's cabin.

Their saddlehorses, a small chestnut and a nervous sorrel, were tethered in the woods about 300 yards from the corral, the churned-up ground showed clearly where a third rider had left at speed. Both animals wore Stobley's Boxed S brand

and the saddles were similarly marked. So the men had probably come into Denver with Benteen on the Union Pacific, from Pacerville I supposed.

I fed and grained the horses and turned them out with the bay. They seemed to know each other so I left them to it. Returning again to the cabin I made myself a fresh pot of coffee and opened a tin of peaches which I ate with a knife.

Neither of the dead men's pockets contained much of any value. They had one clasp knife each, one pocket-watch and fifteen dollars between them. The watch belonged to Wilcox. The weapons were another matter. Wilcox had a near matched pair of Colt .45s, both short-barrelled and both in fine condition. One he had worn in a shoulder holster which the shotgun blast had ruined and the other in a tooled leather holster, the shellbelt for which would have gone around my slim waist once and then half way again. Bobby Lattimer's handgun was a pearl-handled, double-action Smith & Wesson Frontier in .44-40 calibre. Not that unusual but rare enough to be of interest to me. He carried it in a scruffy hand-me-down holster that had at one time seen service with the US Army, the flap having been cut away many years before. The shellbelt was scuffed and many of the loops torn away, the nine that were still intact carried brass shells for the Smith.

Killing had never set easy with me, not before the war as a young peace officer, not during the war and not after it. I had taken Lattimer and Wilcox down with the casual coldness so necessary in a gunfight of any kind. My aim had been to survive and I had. But it did not end there and it had not ended with the burying of the two men. Their lives, like others before them, were now part of me, part of my trappings to be hauled around wherever I went. I would think about them from time to time, remember them and the moment they had fallen and be glad that it had not been me. If I had learned only one certain thing in the war then it was the fact that the dead do not go away. Neither your own dead companions or your dead enemies ever really leave this earth. The something of them that lives on in the memory is, in part, their immortality. The faces of dead comrades often smiled out at me from a flickering campfire and sometimes, on misty summer evenings, I had seen the faceless, anonymous men in grey uniforms crossing my pony's track, as far away from me then as they had been when I had killed them with a Minié ball at 70 yards or driven a bayonet through their hearts when their faces had been inches from my own but obscured by the powdersmoke and my tears.

# FIVE

As promised Jack Brubaker returned on Friday afternoon and he made no comment when I stepped out from behind the privy with the half-cocked shotgun in my hand as he rode into the yard.

'Hunting,' I said lamely.

'Hunting,' he repeated, turning his broad back toward me and leading his horse over to the corral. He looked at the two new arrivals and then at me. 'We got visitors, Wes?'

'We had some,' I replied.

'Where are they now?' he asked, looking at me, curiosity nagging at him but trying not to show it.

'Down by the creek, five or six feet under. Floating around in muddy water I shouldn't wonder.'

'You want to tell me about it?' he asked, stripping his saddle from the horse and leading it into the corral.

'Yes, sure. You get my stuff?'

'I did and the bay is yours at a good price.' He tossed me a secondhand but good-looking Winchester carbine and hefted a gunnysack and canvas bag from behind his saddle. I followed him up to the cabin watching as he paused to examine the freshly chipped timber around the bullet holes in the door.

'Thank you for that,' I said.

'You're welcome. Lattimer and Wilcox?'

'And George Benteen.'

'You get them all?' he asked over his shoulder, walking in through the cabin's open doorway.

'Not Benteen. I didn't see George, just heard him giving his orders out there in the woods.'

'How did they come at you?' He was looking at me with a slightly amused look on his sad face.

'Caught me out in the open without any pants on but they were not very good and I made it back inside. You want some coffee, it's freshly made?'

He nodded and I poured two mugs of steaming black Joe. 'Young Bobby hid out behind the privy and Wilcox tried to creep up behind the cabin. He aimed to blindside me I guess.'

'You found the port, obviously.'

'Yeah, took Wilcox down with both barrels of your scattergun. Hoped to get Bobby to lay down his firearm but you know the way it goes, Jack, he had to try.'

'Shotgun again?'

'Choked barrel only. He was a boy really.'

'He was big enough, mean enough and old enough to come after you, Wes, he would have killed you if he had been able. Coffee's damn good. I made some on the ride out here but this is better. There's a warrant out on Wilcox for some damned thing or other.'

'Leave it be, Jack, I'm not going to dig him up so's you can tote him into Denver.'

'No need to, I'll take your word on it. Lawful

killing on Wilcox, whatever, and from the bullet holes in my door, provocation and self-defence where Lattimer is concerned. I'll notify the Arapahoe County sheriff's office.'

'I might have just snuck on the pair of them and bushwhacked them.'

'You could have but I know better and don't forget I was there when Benteen warned you they were aiming to kill you. I wonder what George will do. Does he know you know he was out here?'

'Yes, he knows.'

'Interesting to hear his side of it should I catch up with him. I brought back the things you asked for.'

He tipped the gunnysack out on to the cleared table top. The holster was similar to the one I already owned only longer to accommodate the seven and a half-inch barrel of the .45 Colt Peacemaker. The pistol was brand new straight from the factory and would need some work on it. Brubaker read my mind and grinned.

'I had old Hoagy Smith go over it for you. She's tuned to perfection. I put a couple of rounds through it on the way out here and cleaned it afterwards. It shoots true to forty yards. Further than that is up to the shooter. Here, present for you.' He reached into the wide canvas bag he had carried in along with the gunnysack and produced a stiff, pre-formed, high-crowned black Stetson hat. 'You do look like something in the one you're wearing now, Wes, don't think I could take another day of it.'

I set it on my greying hair and looked in the small brass-framed mirror; it was a good hat, made me look taller. It fitted well too.

\* \* \*

On Saturday morning we walked down to the creek with some empty tin cans and shot them full of holes. Neither of us was much impressed with the Smith & Wesson but it had not been well maintained so it may have been that particular piece and not the Frontier model in general. Wilcox's single actions were a smooth pair and I gave them to Brubaker who seemed much pleased with them and said he would take the Smith to Denver and maybe get it worked on. I kept the few remaining .44-40 shells to go with the carbine he had brought me. The long-barrelled Colt was something else though.

The pistol was smooth to draw and easy to point and shoot. It took a while to get used to the extra two inches of barrel but once I had allowed for them I could get the pistol out very quickly. It shot straight and to Brubaker's amusement I practised from several different angles. Rolling and firing. Running and firing, sending the cans bouncing away. Left and right hand. Kneeling, falling, lying down. I rarely missed and when I did it was only by the merest fraction. I borrowed some ammunition from Brubaker and tried to draw again. This time it was more fluid, faster and easier on the wrist. I ejected the empties and reloading the piece pushed the weapon back into the crossdraw holster.

'Good job I bought you an extra couple of boxes, Wes, or you would be heading for Wyoming with an empty shellbelt.'

We went fishing on Sunday. Brubaker was an accomplished fisherman and I could roll-cast a lure with a fair degree of accuracy. His beautifully shaped, handmade lures quickly brought hungry trout to the landing nets. We built a fire beside the creek and pan-boiled them in a skillet over the hot ashes their sparkling multi-coloured scales laced with herbs and salt. We ate the fish with our fingers and washed it down with a bottle of wine Brubaker had brought back from Denver. We talked about old times and card games and of men we had both known. Some alive, some retired and many of them dead. In its way it was a melancholy last day together but one we would both remember.

The next morning we packed our gear, saddled our horses and rode away from the cabin and out to the road that would take Brubaker back to his job and me along a trail I had no real choice but to ride. Out across the Medicine Bow River, the North Platte and beyond the Rattlesnake Range to where the foothills of the Big Horn Mountains sweep along and down to the grassland forty miles east of the Powder River Canyon. From there, if I could make it before winter set in, across to the Snake.

'Luck to you, Wes. I'll wire you the reward money and the badge will be here in the spring for you if you want it. I'll guarantee that.' He reached out and shook my hand. 'You ever need me just holler. I got big ears.'

'Thanks for everything, Jack. For this,' I swept my hand out to the free and open range before me, 'and for being there.'

'Glad to be there for you, Wes.'

He turned his big horse off toward Cherry Creek and the distant township of Denver and I watched him out of sight to a bend in the trail. He waved once and I returned the wave holding my hand in the air long after he had gone from my view.

# SIX

It has never been my way to give a pony a human name. I have owned, ridden hard, had shot out from under me six fine horses since I first took to the wearing of a federal badge. I have hired many more, animals of a passing fair nature but quickly forgotten when returned to the livery stables of their origin. The bay was another matter. We got along well together from the very first. Brubaker had told me the horse was called Sonny. I suppose to someone somewhere he had seemed like a Sonny but to me he was a horse, a bay, a surefooted, seemingly tireless animal that could move at an easy pace from sunrise to sundown and still be in a reasonable disposition the following day.

We had covered a lot of ground over some rugged and beautiful country since waving goodbye to Jack Brubaker that morning and, pushing the bay hard, eager to leave Colorado behind me, we crossed Boxelder Creek south of the Wyoming border just before sunset.

I pulled the bay to a stop on a small ridge overlooking the green valley. The sun was low, casting deep shadows where the ground fell away into grassy dips. The creek itself ran red with the setting of the sun and along its western bank a small herd of buffalo grazed away the last of the daylight. It was a lovely sight. In many ways I have never been able to understand the white man's stupidity and greed even though I am one of their kind. On many of the central plains south of Kansas and into Texas the buffalo have all but gone, fallen under the Sharps rifles carried by many of the hunters.

I watched the huge shaggy animals drink their bellies full and then vanish like ghosts into the long grass and the mist that hovered above the river and the surrounding grassland.

The bay picked its way down to the water's edge and drank. I refilled my canteen and by the very last glow of the early autumn twilight I made my camp beside a fallen willow tree, its short thick trunk protecting both me and the fire from the fresh northerly breeze, bearable when diluted by the daylight's bright sunshine but chillingly cold in the darkness of the night.

We made even better time the following day, that bay pony and me. We crossed the Wyoming border, skirted Cheyenne and clipped on north-wards camping that evening ten or twelve miles to the north of the Laramie River. I made my camp on open ground and kept a small fire of buffalo chips burning all through the night to keep a chill out of my bones that the hot coffee of my supper had failed to disperse. My body ached all over, unused as it was to the strain of the activity demanded of it but the pain was easing daily.

Four long days after riding out of the cabin's yard and crossing Cherry Creek and following my last night camp on the Deer Creek Range, I crossed the south fork of the Powder River and crested the final hill between myself and my old home, the Diamond H Ranch.

It was late afternoon when I rode down that familiar hunting trail, along Blackwater Creek and around the bend to the ranch house. I pushed the bay through the broken gate and into the hardpacked dirt yard. The place was burned to the ground, derelict and deserted. The main building was a mess of charred timber broken free and hanging loose against the scorched uprights, creaking in the breeze, groaning out a welcome to me. The veranda was still pretty much intact although the planking was scorched and lifted in places, twisted away the big steel nails rusted and bent. Arising from the left side of the ruin was the dressed-stone chimney still whole and ready for a fire.

The corral was broken down and of the barn, the small bunkhouse and the feedshack nothing was left other than piles of black woodash teased by the wind and drifting out into the yard. The windmill was still standing and the watertank filled with fresh water. The soil was littered with cow chips, rutted and turned by a thousand passing hooves. Cattle had been here many times and recently but of man there was no sign other than the fact that the windmill did not creak on its freshly oiled bearings.

I dismounted and tied the bay off to a broken hitching rail. Combing the ground and the debris I found where a gunshot had split a rail fence and where many more gunshots had hit the timbers of the main building including the porch floor. But I could find nothing else. I swung back up on to the bay and pushed it through the failing light to where the creek wandered out from a stand of willow trees. I made camp there keeping a low fire, eating beef jerky and drinking hot, sweet coffee.

Perhaps it was the coffee, the cold or a combination of both but I could not sleep. I moved my bedroll closer to the campfire and pulled the sack of Bull Durham that Brubaker had insisted on my taking, out of a saddle-bag. Shaking some tobacco into a yellow paper I rolled a cigarette and lit it with a glowing twig of firewood.

I pushed some more fuel on to the fire and placed the smoky refilled coffee-pot among the embers, thinking, wondering what might have happened here. In the meantime all that I could do was keep warm and try to remember it as it had once been.

My father had not become a cattleman by design and we were not from the Territories. We were Texans. I was born, raised and educated in the town of Rio Brazos, South Texas, where cooling winds drift in from the saltwater sea and keep the hot afternoons at a comfortably cool temperature.

I was nearly twenty years old when my parents moved north-west to Missouri and already a lawman, a Texas Ranger riding in the company of Captain John Coffee Hays. I had no dream other than to be a peace officer. My father nurtured his own hidden dream that I would eventually tire of riding dusty trails, fighting Indians and badmen, 'with that Goddamned lump of iron on your hip and a Mex coin pinned on your chest'. I carried a hefty .44 Walker Colt and the Mexican coin he referred to was my Ranger badge, the star set in a circle was, like so many, fashioned from a Mexican silver five peso coin.

In '55, when my mother died, I quit the Texas Ranger Force and moved to St Joseph to help my father who himself was very ill with the fever that had killed my mother. It took four months for him to fully recover during which time I had taken a deputy sheriff's job in Dandelos County. He used to joke that if he ever lost me he knew he could always count on finding me behind one badge or another. And I guess he was right about that.

Tired of Missouri and with my sorely begrudged help he sold up again and moved to Wyoming Territory. With his not inconsiderable savings he built up a small ranch naming it the Diamond H. He put cattle on the rich grass-covered range together with a healthy remuda of horses. He had no burning ambition to be a cattle baron and was happy with his narrow valley, its natural boundaries of rugged Big Horn foothills and endless water supply. Like always, as soon as he was set I accepted an offered deputy US marshal's badge and worked out of Fort Morgan in Colorado and that was where I had first met Jack Brubaker.

Although most of my Texas colleagues would not have approved, when the expected Civil War became a dreadful reality and the blood of Bull Run was barely dry I joined the Union Army. Serving first in the cavalry and then, soon after the horror of Fredricksburg where I was set afoot, I was seconded to the provost marshal's staff as a lieutenant working directly out of the War Department in Washington.

My father wrote me a letter at about that time, a

letter that I treasure yet. In it he told me that he loved me and respected my choice of careers. He told me of his hope that although I would not be inclined to run the ranch, I would always consider it to be my home. I made him that promise and, when the surrender was signed at Appomattox Court House, I returned to Wyoming in the company of an elderly Negro named Moke Calloway who had worked in the provost marshal's office as a courier and later as one of my assistants. He was born to be around cattle and the two old men got on like a brushfire.

I wondered where Moke and Florence his wife were this night. I asked the bay hobbled close by but he only snorted and loudly broke wind.

# SEVEN

I awoke stiff and cold with my left leg aching. That happened from time to time especially if I slept badly and I had slept badly. Bob Deacon's West Texas bullet had done a great deal of damage to my thigh muscles, much more so to the left than to the right leg. The fire was out and the eastern horizon was slightly lighter than the sky above it. I could hear cattle bawling, it had been that which had awakened me with such a start. I stamped the cold and the ache out of my legs and walked clear of the willow trees.

There were maybe eighty to a hundred head of cattle making their way in from the range and down to the yard of the Diamond H, driven by two weary looking drovers with scarves tied tightly over their hats crushing the brims to their cold ears. With my arms wrapped around me and my cold hands buried in my armpits I stayed hidden and watched as the cowhands turned back the way they had come and some of the steers drank at the well while others dirtied the creek above my camp sending muddy water running past me.

All of the cattle that I was close enough to see were wearing the Barking Dog iron an unusual brand and one that I was unfamiliar with. It was shaped in the crude profile of a wolf-like dog with an open mouth. I waited until the waddies were out of sight then I cleared my camp, emptied the cold coffee on to the dead fire and saddled the bay. Blackwater was only seven miles down the trail, I would take a proper breakfast there. Maybe at the Bluebird Café if it was still in business.

Blackwater Creek had changed considerably in the few years since I had last been there. It still lay in a misty little valley about 300 yards or so away from the deep running creek and this cold morning the mist was deepened by a low lying, sweet-smelling woodsmoke.

The changes were quite obvious. What had once been a single main street running north to south with a few decrepit, false-fronted buildings facing on to it was now three times as long with a slightly narrower cross street bisecting it about half-way down. The main street itself split into a Y shape at the northern end with the two forks bending to the left and right after about fifty yards with one fork ending at a schoolyard and the other at a freshly painted white church. In the island left by the forks was an impressive, partially brick built, long-porched town hall which included the town jail together with the mayor's and sheriff's offices. Most of the new buildings were well kept and neatly painted with several businesses appearing to have only recently opened.

A gunsmith and sporting goods dealer had taken over what had been the site of the small general store which itself had been re-sited at twice the size next to the Stockman's Bank. The painted sign proclaimed it to be Belowen's Dry Goods and Clothing Store. I noticed it was not the only business to sport the name of Belowen. The name also decorated a real estate office, an assay office and a feed store. The barber shop offered ten cent shaves, a haircut for a quarter and a bath for seventy-five cents. There was a telegraph office next to a Wells Fargo and general post office, several boarding-houses and eating-places of various sizes. A Chinese laundry, an undertakers, a boot and shoemakers, a newspaper office – *The Blackwater Standard* – the Union Bakery, a lumber yard and a millinery.

The one spit and sawdust saloon, Harmon David's Buffalo Head, one of the first buildings ever to be erected in Blackwater had grown considerably in width and I guessed depth to become the Harmon David's Cattleman's Rest, what appeared to be a combination saloon and hotel. I also passed a beer hall on the edge of town close by the livery and saw that liquor was served in the Billiards Parlour.

I noted with some relief that the Bluebird Café, although now covering two storefronts, was still operating. I also noted that Aaron Shiffner, the one-time county attorney, now had his own business and his shingle bearing the legend Attorney at Law hung close by to Theresa's father's, Doctor Meyer MD. I wondered if Theresa was up at that hour having breakfast with her husband and Jonah and I also wondered for the tenth time since leaving the ruin of my own father's ranch if coming into Blackwater was such a good idea.

A large livery stable and barn stood at the

southern end of the town and opposite to that several well-maintained stockyards. I could only guess at what the other street had to offer.

Riding along the near deserted main drag at just after seven in the morning it was plain to see that a man could almost walk clear from one end of Blackwater Creek to the other on a rainy day and not get his hat wet or his boots muddy. the close-boarded, portico-covered sidewalk ran the complete length of the street broken only by the odd alleyway or the new crossover street. Money had come to the town and, I guessed from the number of businesses with livestock affiliations, cattle could be the reason for the boom. And yet with all the enterprise there was an air of emptiness and desolation about the place as if the boom had not quite happened.

Blackwater Creek had the feel of a fairground, the booths open and waiting, the grifters ready and eager to count the dollar bills, a whore all painted and powdered, dressed up and waiting for the darkness and her first customer.

I tied the bay off at the hitching rail outside of the Bluebird Café next to a small pinto wearing a Barking Dog mark on its hip and walked in through the half-open door. One other customer, a trail hand, was sitting at the narrow counter. The place smelled of bacon grease and old tobacco smoke. I slid into a booth and waited. After a moment or two a slim, redheaded woman came to my table to take my order. I gave it to her. Three eggs sunnyside up, bacon, hash, beans, biscuits and coffee. Lots of coffee. The woman cleared some dirty plates and a mug from the table without ever looking at my face which gave me time to study hers without appearing to be rude.

Her name was Kelly Doohan and although I knew her to be around thirty years old she looked nearer to forty. Her hands were worn and cracked from too many hours immersed in hot water and her face was deeply lined around the full mouth and green eyes. She still had the remains of a dark bruise under one eye. I had known her quite well, even kissed her and rolled in the hay with her on one occasion, a Saturday night long before I had met Theresa Meyer. She scribbled my order, just another scruffy cowboy in for a hot breakfast before the cold day's work began.

Perhaps that is how anyone else I might run into who knew me would see me or rather how they would not see me. It was a useful non disguise my four day growth, dirty canvas jacket and scarred stovepipe chaps. Just another drifter in for a hot cup of Joe. It was something to consider and I kept my new hat on.

The breakfast was good and hot and the biscuits quite special. I drank two cups of coffee and dropped some coins on to the table leaving enough for a generous tip. Perhaps that was a mistake. I was at the door and watching her in the large mirror. She picked up the money, counted it and looked curiously at my departing back. She was still looking, searching her mind for something when I swung back up on the bay and headed down the street toward the livery stable. A boy took the pony with a nod and the quarter with a smile. The quarter I told him was for taking extra special care of my horse. To feed the animal and give it a good rub down. I also asked him to get the blacksmith to check out his shoes. He asked me how the horse was called and I said the bay did not have a name.

It was nearly 8.30 and Blackwater was stirring. The clerk at the general store was rolling a barrel out on to the sidewalk and several locks were being turned and open signs displayed although the main street was still deserted.

Leaning against the livery's corral fence I considered my options. I needed information and that would be from the sheriff or one of the gabby businessmen on main street. Experience has long since taught me that the gabbiest man in any town is usually the barber and that would be my first port of call. The law would be my second. I put aside my fears of being recognized.

Leaving my bedroll in the livery but carrying my Winchester, saddle-bags and the carpetbag I had exchanged with Brubaker for my leather valise, I walked along the street to the barber shop. The proprietor, a balding, pock-faced, short-statured man in sleeve garters, striped shirt, black pants and white apron, was just opening for business. He looked surprised and more than a little pleased at so early a customer.

I nodded, pushed my way past the man whom I did not recognize and dumped my gear on to the slatted bench which ran the length of the room's back wall.

'Good morning, sir, what'll it be?' he asked, pointing to the new polished steel and leather-backed chair rubbing his hands together like they were cold. In fact the room was warm and I guessed a furnace out back was heating the day's bath water.

'The works, mister, a shave, haircut, bath and one of those five-cent cheroots to smoke while I soak.'

'Yes, sir,' he said, delighted at the range of my

needs, taking my dirty canvas jacket holding it at arm's length and hanging it on a bentwood coat and hat-rack. I sat down and he tilted back the chair setting it at the right height before placing hot towels on my stubble-laden cheeks. 'You'll excuse me, sir, I'll organize the bath while you sit awhile and relax there under the hot towels.'

There is something special about being shaved by an expert and the sign over the door claimed John Long to be an expert. And that was no lie.

Straightening the chair he handed me a towel and asked how I'd like my hair. I had not been asked that question for a long time. In prison you got what the man gave you.

'Trim it around the ears, John, and keep it short.'

'Sure thing. You're a stranger around here aren't you? First visit to Blackwater Creek?' he asked, snipping at the ends of my hair putting right what the careless prison barber had put wrong. John Long, setting out to learn all that he could from me in order to pass it along to the next customer and get through his day, living on words and information.

'No, I've been here before, a long time ago. It was smaller then as I recall. Hobe Duff was the barber back then. What happened to him, he die?'

'No, Hobe was too damned mean to peg out, he just sold out. To me. I bought him out lock, stock and bath tubs,' he laughed to himself. 'He left a little too soon as I see it.'

'How come,' I asked.

'Well, like you said, mister, back then Blackwater was a dump. A speck of fly crap on the map of Wyoming Territory but now it's going to be something.'

'It is?'

'You can bet on it.'

'Railroad coming through?'

'That and a lot more. Cattle, mister. This country is going to boom with cattle. We got plenty now and in the spring there are going to be a lot more. Big herds moving in from Texas and Kansas. We fatten them here and sell them on.'

'Beef?'

'As far as you can see come the next few years. With the buffalo all gone the Indians, the army and the railroad need feeding. Not to mention the wagon trains passing through to the south of here. Hungry people.'

'When is all of this going to happen, John? I see plenty of cows out on the range already.'

'Many more to come, sir, and Blackwater Creek will boom. You can put your last dollar on that. I have.'

'Who's organizing this bonanza I ought to get in on?'

'The Belowen Cattle Company. Tom Belowen, owner of the Barking Dog, the biggest spread around here, hell, about the only spread around here, he's seen to it we boom.'

'I have seen a lot of boomtowns, gold, cattle, copper, coal, even sheep but they usually boom when the boom's booming if you get my drift. They don't ordinarily set themselves up to meet a need but boom because of that need.'

'Stick around, my friend, it's going to happen come the spring. You can take that to the bank.'

He brushed off my dirty shirt collar and asked me pointedly if I was changing my clothes in the bath house, did I want my dirty ones collected. 'The Chink from the laundry collects and delivers back to your hotel. Where're you staying?'

'Where would you recommend, John?' I asked getting out of the chair and unstrapping my gunbelt.

'Depends on how you're fixed.'

'I'm fixed pretty good and yes I would like my dirty laundry collected.'

'Then I would suggest maybe the Cattleman's would suit you. It's across from the telegraph office.'

'Thanks. I'll give it a try. Bath about ready?'

'Sure thing.' I paid him for the haircut and the bath. He extracted a slim cigar from the humidor and handed it to me. 'On the house, you promise to call again.'

I nodded my thanks, took my black hat off the peg and picking up my bag and gunbelt walked through the curtained doorway and out back into the large bath house. It smelled of wet earth, hot water and scented soap. There were five enormous wooden half-barrels set close together on slatted duckboarding with a wooden bench between each barrel. There was a clean blue striped towel on each bench. One of the barrels was filled near to the brim with steaming water.

Half-way through the cigar a small pigtailed Chinaman in a long white linen coat and with a round black pillbox of a hat on his head bowed his way into the bath house and picked up my soiled clothes. I asked him did he clean boots and he bowed even lower and disappeared from the room with them. I hoped he was bright enough to bring the boots back to the bath house and not take them over to the Cattleman's Hotel.

I soaked and I smoked and when the dirty,

scummy water got too cold for comfort I hauled
myself out and towelled my body and hair dry. The
clean clothes were badly creased but they would
shake out quickly I supposed. My town-wear, the
black woollen pants – not worn since before my
arrest – fitted fairly snugly as did the black vest but
the grey shirt was a little loose around the collar so
I left it open and instead of the lace tie I cornered a
big red polkadot handkerchief and tied it around
my throat with the big point to the front. I slapped
the gunbelt around my waist setting the holster
with the grip toward my middle and wiped the
steamy mirror clear to check the results. I doubt
that anyone would have recognized me as the dirty,
trail-weary rider of breakfast time in the Bluebird
Café. Maybe not even Kelly Doohan. However
there was one dark cloud on my horizon. The
Chinaman had not returned my boots assuming
quite reasonably but nevertheless quite wrongly,
that I had another pair.

I thanked the barber, promised to call back the
next day for another shave and left his shop
walking in my thickly stockinged feet three doors
along to the boot and shoemakers. The air was still
cold and the weak sun made little impression on
the chill morning air. Promising myself a thick new
canvas jacket to combat the cold, I stepped in
through the doorway and came face to face with a
handsome woman in a long floral patterned dress.
Theresa Meyer or Shiffner as I now supposed her
to be.

# EIGHT

Her sudden appearance took me by surprise but I could see by the startled look on her face, the colouring of her cheeks, that my walking in through the doorway of the shop had taken her by even greater surprise. She froze as did I. We stared at each other. I suppose that I had known all along that a chance meeting in what was still a small community was inevitable. What I had not bargained for was that the meeting would be quite so soon. I took off my hat playing for time trying desperately to find the words that would make the moment all right, bearable to the both of us. I could not find them but Theresa did.

'Hello, Wesley, it has been a long, long time.' She offered me her hand and I took it, holding it not wanting to let go in case she vanished with it.

'A very long time, Theresa,' I cleared my throat and she gently, almost reluctantly, pulled her hand away from mine, her green eyes moistening. A short, birdlike, middle-aged woman glided up to her side and stared up at me.

'Mrs Belowen,' said Theresa softly, 'this is an old friend of mine, Wesley Harper, he used to be a US marshal from around here.'

Mrs Belowen did not offer me her hand, merely chirped and continued to fix her beady eyes on me as though she was looking for something. Her gaze was piercing and had I known what she was seeking I would have given it up with pleasure and relief.

'I was so sorry to hear about your father, Wes, he was a kind man; Jonah and I were very fond of him,' said Theresa sadly.

'And he of you. How is the boy?'

'Growing taller every day. He will want to see you.'

It was a flat enough statement, pleasing in its way but seeming to mean more. I was too confused to reach out for it.

'I came back to see Moke Calloway. I came by way of the ranch,' I said, as if that explained everything there was to know in heaven and upon the earth.

'I'm sorry about that as well, Wes. Things are not now as they once were around Blackwater.'

Again I felt she was saying more to me than the words conveyed and again I passed it by.

'Do you know where I might find him, Theresa?' I enjoyed saying her name aloud. I had spoken it softly in the darkness to myself many times over the years.

'He boards at the Bell House now, it's a small boarding-house on Belowen Street.' She thought for a moment and added gently, 'He's a widower and a cripple now, Wes.'

'Belowen Street?'

'Named after my husband,' said the little woman quietly her gaze shifting from my face to my collar, to my pistol belt and right down to the floor. 'You have no shoes on Mister Harper.'

'I left the hotel in a hurry,' I said, by way of an explanation.

I looked directly into Theresa's pale-green eyes and tried a smile. For a brief instant the smile was returned.

'Then you have come to the right store, sir, my husband owns it and it has a fine range of footwear; buy yourself a spare pair why don't you. Come, Theresa, we must be going, George will be waiting.' She walked past me and out through the still open doorway.

'Are you going to be in Blackwater for long, Wes?'

'I may well be, I don't really know yet but it was good to see you.'

Theresa touched my arm her hand lingering for a moment. 'Goodbye, Wes, it was good to see you too.'

And then she was gone leaving me standing there with my cold feet, my thundering heart and trembling knees, very aware that there had not been a wedding ring on her slim white finger.

I purchased a pair of soft black leather boots paying more than I really wanted to spend but aware of the fact that comfortable boots usually came expensive and that there was no substitute for happy and contented feet.

From the boot shop I went to the general store and bought a fleece-lined canvas jacket, deerskin gloves and obtained the free direction from the talkative clerk that Belowen Street was the eastern arm of the new road crossing the main street which, as far as I could tell, was still known as Main Street.

The Bell House was a clean and well-kept two storey building. The clerk, a red-faced Irishman, looked me up and down and extracted as much information from me as he was going to get before telling me that Moke Calloway was in room seven at the back of the ground floor and that he was one mean old black son-of-a-bitch until after he had eaten his midday meal. I told him I thought I could handle his meanness and walked along the corridor he indicated. I knocked on the door numbered seven and waited.

'Get the hell out of my face,' a deep, rasping voice answered my knock.

I opened the door and went in. The old Negro, Moke Calloway, was sitting in a stuffed armchair a pair of crutches resting on the chair's arm. He looked at me but did not speak. Waiting. He was rail thin and wasted. His cheeks were sunken, his neck scrawny and by the dusty pale light drifting in through the curtained window I could see that he was nearly if not totally blind in one eye. 'Who's that?' he asked producing a huge Dragoon Colt and pointing it in my general direction.

'It's me, Moke, Wes Harper, and for God's sake put up that cannon.'

A childlike smile of delight leaped across his thin face revealing a wide mouth filled with yellowing teeth.

'Oh Lord in heaven, Wesley Harper, the Shadow Rider. Sweet Jesus, boy, I have waited a long year for you to come home to me.' And then he was crying.

# NINE

The old Negro was pleased to see me and desperate to talk but his words were all strung together, a jumble of confusion, often garbled and punctuated by fits of coughing. On more than one occasion he referred to me as my father and it took a while before I had him calmed down enough to structure a conversation. I quietened him down and with a degree of argument coupled with some good old-fashioned down-home bribery I persuaded him to leave the boarding-house and join me for a drink in one of the saloons on Main Street. I hoped that being away from that drab room out in the fresh air would help him in some way to reassess his flimsy grip on my reality. With a good deal of effort I got him dressed and wrapped in his old blue Union Army overcoat into one deep pocket of which he insisted upon sliding the big Colt Dragoon. He also insisted on taking both his crutches rather than rely on my arm.

Watched closely by the Irish desk clerk we walked out through the lobby of the boarding-house and made our way along to the water-hole of his choice, Brown's Beer Hall, half-way down Main and nearly opposite the barber shop. We stopped once on the way in order for me to dodge into the Cattleman's Hotel, to register and advise them of the imminent return of my laundry.

The midday sun was warm and comforting holding the winter at bay. The air still heavily scented with woodsmoke was clear and the sky a cold ice blue. John Long stepped out from his barber shop to watch our passing, he nodded and I guessed was bristling inside with curiosity. Long was not the only person on the near deserted street to take an interest in the progress of me and the old black man as we thumped along Main Street's sidewalk, me in my new boots and Moke on his crutches. A stout man dressed in a long dark overcoat and with a black patch over his left eye watched us from the doorway of the feed store. I held his good eye until it wavered and he looked down to examine his fingernails.

Brown's Beer Hall was the spit and sawdust drinking place that the Buffalo's Head had once been. A long oiled-pine bar with several stools in front of it ran the length of one wall and an unpolished and darkly tarnished brass footrail ran its full length with equally tarnished cuspidors stationed like dirty-faced sentries at each end. A half-dozen tables were fighting for space on the raw-timbered and spur-scarred floorboards. A large black potbellied stove was the only real concession to comfort although I rather doubted it would have much effect when the mean winter really hit northern Wyoming.

Apart from a jar of uninviting pickled eggs floating in dirty, yellowy-green vinegar Brown's offered food of sorts with the day's offering chalked on to a board behind the long bar. I

ordered two beef stews and two beers from the
bartender, a bewhiskered red-faced man with
slicked-down hair, bad teeth, black fingernails and
a filthy shirt. His long white apron was none too
clean either and thinking about it I cancelled the
food and stuck to the beer telling Moke we could
get a meal in the Bluebird Café later on. He said he
didn't care much for the Bluebird Café and I told
him that if he felt strongly about it then we could
eat someplace else.

I sipped a single beer to Moke's two. He was into
his third before he spoke and it was as if the old
Moke of my army days had never gone away, had
just been hiding behind the tired old eyes of the
man now surfacing through the beer, freed by the
alcohol.

'Your daddy missed you sure enough, boy,' he
said after a while. He was not speaking directly to
me but, because of his failed eyesight he appeared
to be addressing someone a little to the left of my
shoulder.

'I missed him as well, Moke. He came to Denver
once in a while and we had a visit or two in other
places.'

'He visit with you in Washington, said you
introduced him to the President of these United
States. Sure must have been something to see, you
and your daddy and old Sam Grant talking
together like that.' He chuckled wetly.

'I stopped by the ranch on my way into town,
Moke, it's all burned up. What happened out
there?' I changed the subject not ready to talk
about my father to anyone yet. Also, although I did
not want to frighten him back inside himself, I was
impatient to know what had happened at the ranch

and perhaps that impatience was noticeable in the thin edge of my voice. He was silent for a long while sipping his beer looking past me.

'What happened to Florence, Moke?'

'She got burned with the house, Wesley. Shot clean through the head when they come to burn us out. Killed the dog too.'

'Who came to burn you out, Moke?'

'It was dark when they come shooting and burning, shot Florence clear through the head and I left her there lying on the floor and ran. They got me though. Shot me all over. Crippled me. Would have died hadn't been for your woman, Theresa and her doctor daddy.'

My woman. I let it pass but it felt good for a moment and I wondered about that ringless finger.

'You have no idea as to the who or the why, Moke?'

Suddenly he stared right into my eyes leaning across the table, spittle drooling down the side of his mouth. 'The deputy was one of 'em, him and the 'breed calls hisself Santana, but I didn't say nothing about knowing anything before you come back and take care of it. There was plenty of others and sometimes I remember them and sometimes I just plain forget.'

He sat back in his chair again, composed, drinking his beer and wiping his lips with the rough woollen sleeve of his overcoat.

He said little more of anything that made much sense to me. He was an old man, I had no real way of knowing if what he said happened actually had happened. It somehow seemed unlikely that anyone would burn down the Diamond H let alone kill his wife. Maybe he had knocked an oil lamp over, or perhaps Florence's cooking got out of hand. They were a very old couple and in some way I felt responsible for them having been placed in a position of danger. On the other hand he could well be remembering it as it actually was. I needed another source.

Moke refused my offer of a meal and at some point in a conversation that was becoming more and more one-sided he struggled to his feet, picked up his crutches and walked out of the beer hall in mid-sentence saying something about a dead horse. Thumping across the room leaving me there with an unfinished beer and as many questions as I had had when I first rode into Blackwater.

Mark Newell was the county sheriff or, at least he had been when I left the area in order to take up my position in Washington. Blackwater isn't the county seat and although he spent a great deal of time there the permanent day-to-day maintenance of law and order was entrusted to a deputy of his choosing. I could not remember who had been in office when I had left but assumed it did not really matter as the job changed hands fairly frequently. I left Brown's and made my way northward up Main Street toward the town hall and the sheriff's office there. It was eerie walking that deserted street with its stores, its saloons and places of business all open and ready for the rush of customers that never came. I crossed Belowen Street and made my way along to where the newly painted town hall stood in isolated splendour its Union flag hanging limp in the still, early afternoon air. The sheriff's office was just inside and to the left of the entrance with its barred window looking out on to and down the

full length of Main Street. I pushed in through the
half-glazed door and stopped.

Like the rest of the town the office was newly
decorated and the furniture, a deep pedestal desk,
chairs, small bookcase and large rifle and shotgun
cabinet with the weapons neatly chained through
their trigger-guards was not the rough and ready
equipment usually associated with a frontier lawman's office. The room was bright enough but it
stank of a badly kept oil lamp and tobacco smoke.

The man sitting behind the desk was the same
man who had watched my progress earlier as Moke
and I had made our way to the beer hall. He no
longer wore the long coat or the wide-brimmed tan
hat. The missing hat revealed close-cropped brown
hair and the discarded overcoat showed a deputy's
badge pinned to a dark vest and a holstered Colt .45
with fancy mother-of-pearl grips slung on a shellbelt around his wide hips. He looked up as I entered
the room, a heavily jowled face with a bushy moustache under a hooked nose. There was white scar
tissue running in a jagged line down his cheek for
two inches below the black patch. He fixed me with
the one diamond-sharp black eye.

'You would be Wes Harper if I'm not mistaken.'
His voice was deep, the words spoken slowly and
with great care. He sounded like a man who weigh-
ed out each and every word before speaking, even
rehearsing whatever it was he was going to say
before actually saying it.

'You are not mistaken, Deputy, and you are …?' I
left it hanging there.

'Chase Hawkins, county deputy. what can I do for
you, Harper?'

He did not offer to shake hands so I left mine

jammed into the pockets of my new jacket.

'Just information, Deputy.' I kept my voice flat, not friendly and not hostile, just matter-of-fact. What I did not do was call him sheriff, a courtesy title usually used when talking to a county deputy sheriff in charge of his own town.

'This isn't an information office, Harper, you want to know about the town try the mayor's office.' He looked back down at the fliers he had been reading when I had entered the room peering at the strained faces staring back out at him, seemingly dismissing me. But we both knew I would not be going anywhere for a while. I stood there waiting.

After a long silent moment or two Hawkins looked up at me. 'You still here?'

'You really think your bad attitude is going to scare me away, Deputy?'

'I'm not trying to scare you, Harper, you'll know well enough when that happens. What I'm telling you is I got no time to talk to an ex-jailbird who wanders into my town and into my office without an appointment.'

'Let's drop the jailbird crap right here and now, Deputy,' I let a hard edge slip into my voice so he would be in no doubt that wherever it went from there on I would ride right along with it. All the way. 'I got a full pardon from the governor and an apology from the Supreme Court and I got it in writing.'

He got to his feet leaning forward across his wide desk his weight on the knuckles of his big hands. 'What you got is a piece of dirty paper that don't mean squat to me and what I want is for you to get out of here, out of my office and out of my town.

Now, today, or you could find yourself back behind bars and a long ways from home.'

He had thought those words out, rehearsed them.

'You are forgetting one thing here, Deputy,' I said quietly.

'And just what would that be now?'

'This is my home. I've come back to work my father's ranch and to find out exactly what happened out there. You being the law and all I figured you could tell me, save me a whole mess of time. What you don't tell me others will be happy to and you don't bother me one small bit, Deputy; I've met a whole lot of cheap, tough-talking tin badges like you and not one of them was as fast with a piece as he was with his mouth.' I can be a great and tactful conversationalist when needs must.

He started to come around the desk toward me but stopped at the corner, thinking about it. Like his words, no action without a good deal of thought. Chase Hawkins could be a very dangerous man for that one good reason alone.

'You would do better to ride on and leave it be.'

'Mark Newell still the county badge?' I asked.

Hawkins was thrown by the question but quickly recovered.

'What's it to you?' he asked, the one dark eye trying to read the situation but showing nothing other than the malice that had been there when I first walked into his office.

'He's a good man and I'm wondering what he was thinking of leaving a bucket of wind and horse manure like you in charge.'

I turned on my heel and left the room conscious of the fact that a tiny squeak had developed across the toe of my new boots.

I stood outside on the sidewalk breathing deeply of the clean, fresh air, the anger slowly subsiding. I looked up and down the street and decided it would save a lot of my time and trouble if I went straight for it. I could wander around Blackwater Creek asking questions, annoying the local law, making myself unpopular or I could lay out my wares on a blanket and see who would come to buy.

I recrossed Belowen Street and walked back along Main toward the newspaper office I had passed earlier. A man was coming out of the building as I reached the doorway. A tall man, middle-aged, familiar, we both felt it, he nodded and I stepped to one side to let him pass and walked on in through the open doorway. A clerk wearing a green eyeshade stepped over to the gate and low rail fence separating the main room with its press, its stacked paper and benches of lead type from the small front office. He was an old man, thin, bent, white-haired and wearing wire-rimmed, spectacles. His white shirt sleeves were covered by black arm protectors and the rest of his gaunt frame by a long black apron. 'Yes, sir,' said the man cheerfully, 'and what can we do for you?' He peered up at me realizing I wasn't who he thought I was, not someone familiar. A stranger. Suddenly he was curious.

'How often do you publish?' I asked.

'Depends, mister,' he answered.

'On what?' I asked.

'On a lot of things, like what news we got to publish for one thing.'

'Let me put it to you another way,' I said, 'is your boss in?'

'I am the boss.' He stuck out his inky hand.

'Nathan Cooke, reporter, editor, advertising manager, proofreader, publisher and proprietor.'

We shook hands. 'Wes Harper, I own the Diamond H.'

He leaned forward peering up at me. 'John Harper's boy? I never met your old man but I heard plenty about him. Aaron said you was back in town.'

'Aaron Shiffner?'

'You passed him on the way in, he used to be the county attorney, got his own shingle now.'

'He's aged some since we last met.'

'Like the rest of us, boy, getting older every day just sitting around and waiting.'

'Is it going to be worth it?'

'A lot of people have bet their money on it. I moved out here and set up the *Standard*, wouldn't have done that less'n I thought it was worth it.'

'I wish you well then.'

'Why, you interested in the newspaper business?'

'No, not particularly, I wanted to place an advert. A big one, a half-page maybe.'

Nathan Cooke rubbed his hands together. 'Could cost you two dollars or, perhaps, if there is an editorial angle there we could come to some mutual arrangement.' The old man smelling good copy, hoping for it. 'You got it all written down?'

'I'll tell you what I want and you write it down. I don't much care how it comes out so long as it's clear.'

'Wait there a moment.' There was an air of excitement about him. He went over to a tall, upright, single-seat desk and returned with a yellow pad and a freshly sharpened pencil. 'Shoot.'

'It's simple really. I'm going to run the Diamond

H as a working ranch and this is to notify anyone, and I do repeat, anyone, with cattle running on that land has one week to get 'em off my grass.'

'That it?' He sounded disappointed.

'What did you want, gunfire?'

'It sells newspapers.'

'Who you got around here to buy them?'

'You got a point, Mister Harper.'

'It's going to be a long winter.'

'Don't I know it.'

'Do you know a lot of things, Mister Cooke?'

'Call me Nate, everyone else does and yes, I know about 'most everything that goes on in Blackwater.'

'Do you have any idea how the Diamond H got burned down, Nate?'

The old man looked down at his hands then taking a rag from his hip pocket peeled off his spectacles and wiped them clean, breathing some dampness on to them and tackling a real or imagined blemish.

'Most people know what happened there, Mister Harper.'

'I'm not one of them.'

'After you daddy died old Moke ran the place, caretook it really, and there were those who didn't see why a Negro should sit so pretty when they had to work their backsides off for wages.'

'That old black man worked hard all his life.'

'Maybe so but come one Saturday evening, a group of drunks went out there and burned old Moke out, his wife took a wild round in the head and Moke started shooting and got himself gunned down. That was about the size of it.'

'Where was the law while those good old boys were having their high-time Saturday night?'

'Newell was out of town, his deputy, Chase Hawkins, rode out there but he was too late to stop it. Nobody knew for an absolute certainty who did what and Tom Belowen figured ...

'Belowen?'

'The Barking Dog, some of his hands were involved for certain but he figured the damage was done and as no one knew anything for sure it was best to let it ride. He offered old Moke Calloway compensation, pays for his room at the boardinghouse, his medical bills, like that.'

'That's it? A group of rowdies kill an old Negro woman, cripple her man and burn down my father's ranch and Tom Belowen says let it slide?'

Cooke looked me straight in the eye, the air of excitement and expectation hovering just out of sight behind his clean glasses.

'You reckon he should have done a whole lot more is that it?'

I did not answer but asked instead, 'How long ago did all this happen?'

'Maybe a year, just after I got here, hadn't yet set my press up, couldn't even cover the story.'

I was angry again, I could feel it rising up from somewhere just behind my belt buckle, a bitterness swamping me. I had not heard about the killing or the fire and neither had Brubaker. Someone with a lot of weight had sat on the news and prevented the story from ever reaching me or Denver. I took deep breaths and wiped a cold smile across my face.

'Maybe you should add this to your writing,' I said. 'I find the men who hit my ranch and killed the Negro woman I'll be taking them into the US marshals in Cheyenne. Dead or alive, I don't mind how it goes down.'

'Chase Hawkins won't like that, Mister Harper.'

I put four dollars on the counter. 'There's a lot of things Deputy Hawkins isn't going to like around here from now on. Good day to you, Nate, I'm staying at the Cattleman's tonight, you can find me there if you need me, but I'll be moving back out to the ranch tomorrow.'

'It's all burned down.'

'I'll rebuild it and in the meantime there's always the line-camp shack.'

I left him standing there wanting to say something to me but holding it back. I gave him a moment and then turned and left.

The squeak in my new boot was getting louder.

# TEN

Once again I did not sleep well. My supper, taken in the near empty dining-room of the Cattleman's Hotel, sat heavily on my stomach and the whiskey I had used in liberal measures to wash down the burned steak only made matters worse.

Before eating I had wired Brubaker in Denver asking that he hurry along the Charlie Wilcox reward money. I then opened an account at the new bank and told the manager to expect a draft from Denver within the next few days. The man was bloated and grasping, he had bright moist eyes and a fixed smile. I answered his enquiry as to the source of the expected draft with an equally false smile and left him wondering. I did not like the newcomers to Blackwater Creek, they smelled the stink of money and it was clear to me that they had smelled it sometime somewhere before in their lives. The stink stuck and permeated all of the corners of the town. I wondered if Aaron Shiffner carried the smell and what kind of man was Tom Belowen. I was thinking of Belowen and his reluctance to pursue the truth of the burning of my father's ranch when sleep finally took me in her arms and carried me away to a place where

Theresa Meyer was standing alone, dressed in black, a long veil hiding her crying eyes as she stood before a crumbling gravestone bearing my name.

I arose early the next morning with a headache and a bad frame of mind. I washed and dressed and gulped down a hurried breakfast in the Bluebird Café. A thick-set, bearded man was waiting table and I was relieved that Kelly Doohan was not on duty. As promised I called into the barber shop for a shave and disappointed John Long with a taciturn attitude that eventually shut the little man up. I paid him, helped myself to five ten-cent cheroots and bade him a good day. His hang-dog face brought a smile to my own.

Checking out of the Cattleman's I carried my gear, now contained in two carpetbags, down to the livery stable. The boy was still on duty and volunteered that the blacksmith had reshod the bay and that he had personally taken extra special care of the animal. I gave him two bits and setting the blanket, threw the worn saddle over the pony's back. It seemed pleased enough to see me.

I have always like the countryside surrounding Blackwater and especially the creek trail to my father's ranch. It changes constantly from scrub to cottonwood and willow stands with ponderosa pine clinging to the higher ground. The grass is rich and although I could see that it was short grazed it still promised well for winter feed providing the snow was not too deep. Many of the gullies and small canyons that formed part of the foothills to the majestic Big Horn Mountains of the north would offer shelter for wintering cattle provided there were not too many in number. The land would sustain the cattle as it had the buffalo before them for just as long as the grass would last.

I pushed the bay out from the creek cutting off the meandering bends keeping to a straight line above the burned-out ranch house to the line shack at the very northern end of the property. I rode amongst many cattle all carrying the same Barking Dog brand. I would have to charge Belowen for the grazing rights over the past year and I guessed he would not be too pleased although, as a cattleman he would probably understand and come to a fair price per head of beef. I would offer to take brood stock in place of money that should ease his pain.

I saw several raptors hunting the valleys screaming as they circled endlessly on the thermals above the cold landscape. Once I saw a coyote but he was frightened and, keeping low to the ground, bellied his way into the rocks of a gorge well beyond rifle or pistol range. I would not have fired upon it but I knew of few ranchers who would have been so charitable in their dealings with the animal. My father had taught me 'Never shoot what you cannot eat. There is food and room enough for all on these great plains.' I never ever knew it of him to break that simple rule.

As I rode so the sun rose higher and grew in fullness, yellowing, its colour deepening but never seeming to increase much by way of heat. I was warm and comfortable in my stovepipe chaps and thick jacket.

About two miles to the north of the ranch house I cut south and across a meadow which ended in a small ridge of a hill. I crested it, rode through a wood of young cottonwoods and smelled the sweet unmistakable smell of burning ponderosa pine. I dismounted, tied the bay off to a fallen tree, withdrew the carbine from its scabbard and walked through the trees toward where I knew the line camp to be.

It was a well-constructed cabin which I had helped my father build on one of my infrequent visits home. It was a low log construction the joints packed with mud and topped by a lined turf roof. He had complained that it was too cold in winter and too hot in summer. I had hunted from it a time or two filling his winter larder with white-tailed deer, jack-rabbits and quail. I had also spent several nights there with Theresa as well as our one last summer afternoon. It would be a painful, memory-filled place to pass my time but some of the memories I knew would be pleasurable as well as painful.

Clearing the woods and coming upon the cabin I paused while still in the shelter and shadows of the trees surrounding it. There were four saddle ponies in the small but well-maintained corral and two saddles under the overhead cover of the lean-to built alongside the cabin. Smoke was drifting out through the metal chimney and I guessed the big potbellied stove I had hauled up here in bits was still fully operational.

Before stepping clear of the trees I quietly worked the lever of the carbine sliding a shell from the tubular magazine up and into the breech. Taking the pressure with the ball of my thumb I carefully lowered the hammer to half cock and waited.

I suspected that there were two people in the cabin, cowboys, line riders setting up for the winter. It was not their fault they were settling in on my land and not their own. Question was, I wondered, will they die for it? I doubted it but you never could really tell how far a man will go if he imagines he has been pushed.

I walked across the clearing worked the oiled latch on the door and stepped into the one large room. The two cowboys, fully dressed even down to their hats were seated at the rough wooden table eating a late breakfast of beans and eggs. The closed cabin stank of their stale sweat, ancient tobacco, oil, old leather and food. The men froze and I casually laid the carbine on them, cocking the piece.

Both men stared at me, one the furthest from me, reaching toward a holstered pistol hanging from a chairback.

'There's an easy way and there's a hard way, boys. But ask yourself this, is that breakfast worth dying for?' I gave them an easy smile.

There is a moment at such a time when it can all go wrong. Usually a thoughtless, gut-reacting moment when a threatened man will go for his weapon. I had been here a hundred times before and it was still beyond my prediction. The two cowboys, both young men in their late twenties, brothers I guessed, went through that moment. It passed and my heart slowed and I swallowed the dryness from my throat. The cowboy furthest from me leaned forward on the table and filled his fork with beans. His companion's plate was empty but he kept his hands clear and on the table.

'You want grub, help yourself, mister, we got plenty.' It was the older of the two men who spoke, the one with the empty plate.

'Sorry, boys, it's not like that. You are trespassing on my property and I want you gone. You finish eating if you have a mind to, then go pack your gear and get.'

'Who the hell do you think you are? This is Barking Dog ...'

'No, we are getting along fine so let's not part company with an argument. This here is the Diamond H line camp and I own the Diamond H which makes me right and you wrong.' I felt no anger at the ranchhands but I wanted them gone.

'Mister Belowen ...'

I cut him off short. 'You tell Mister Belowen that I want his cattle off this land. You tell him I'll keep the supplies you toted up here and he can deduct it from the grazing fee.'

'Grazing fee?'

'You heard right, son, now eat your beans and get your gear together.'

I stepped around behind them collecting their revolvers, a pair of Colt .44-40s together with two carbines similar to the one I carried. With my own Winchester in the crook of my left arm and casually covering the pair I emptied their weapons dropping the pistols and the ammunition into an empty flour sack. I tossed the sack on to the table and watched as they thought it all through.

'Don't worry about washing the dishes, boys, I'll take care of it later and tell your boss I'll be riding by in the morning.'

I promised myself an early start the next morning and a ride down to the Barking Dog. I did not intend to spend the winter looking over my shoulder.

# ELEVEN

Viewed from the rise which bounded the southern aspect of the Barking Dog headquarters the ranch house was tranquillity itself. Set in a grove of young cottonwoods the new building was flanked by smaller but none-the-less impressive outbuildings. Bunkhouse, barns, feed stores and corrals. A windmill turned noiselessly in the gentle breeze filling a raised corrugated storage-tank which I guessed fed the water supply to the main living-quarters of the Belowens as well as that of the ranchhands. Ponies swished their tails at the last of the midday autumn flies and a large brown hound dog lay basking in the weak sunshine in the lea of the barn. The dog rolled over and climbed to its feet as I pushed the bay into the empty front yard. It did not bark but merely observed my approach with its head quietly cocked to one side as if listening for a word, a command. The ranch was some ten miles from the Diamond H and had not been built when I had last visited my father.

I reined in the bay close by the hitching rail which ran part way across the front of the veranda'd house and, as is the custom in the West, waited to be invited to dismount. The screen door

creaked open and an old man wearing faded
work-clothes looked out at me and went back
inside. Reappearing moments later, he gruffly
invited me to step down then, as I dismounted he
walked forward and took the bay's reins.

'He's expecting you, been waiting since sun-up.
You sleep in or what?' He threw the words over his
shoulder at me as he walked the bay over to the
water trough.

I bit back a reply and mounted the wooden steps,
opened the heavy door and stepped through into
the main room of the ranch house. I had no time to
take in the detail of my general surroundings. As
soon as I entered the room my eyes were engaged
and held fast by the most startling pair of cold, blue
eyes I have ever seen. They belonged to a short,
stumpy, grey-haired, grey-faced man in a darkly
coloured town suit. He was in his late sixties and
standing with his back to a roaring fire one arm
resting on the thick timber shelf set into the
dressed stone of the wall above the open fireplace.
Posing beneath an oil painting of himself in earlier
years astride a chestnut horse, his plumed hat at a
rakish angle the blue eyes complemented by the
dusty butternut of his Confederate Army uniform
and the faded colour of a ragged Southern flag.
We were alone.

The man waited until he was certain the moment
was milked dry and then stepped away from the
flames his hand held out like a sword thrust. I took
it; it was cold but firm.

'Tom Belowen and you, sir, must be the famous
Western marshal, Wesley Harper late of Colorado
Territorial Prison, a Texan who fought for the
Union. Am I correct, sir?'

I did not answer right away but stared into those cold eyes looking for something I knew I would not find. A spark of warmth or even a glint of humour. In those first few seconds I realized that neither were part of Belowen's make-up and in a way that made my visit the easier.

'I'm Wes Harper but I didn't ride out here to discuss my past with you, Belowen, just to deliver a message.'

'A man who does not waste time is a man to reckon with, Harper. I like that. I even respect it so I won't do you the discourtesy of wasting your time either. I already have your message from my men you sent packing out of the line shack. It was clear and to the point as I will be with you. Drink?'

I shook my head feeling a damned fool standing there with my hat in my hand being talked down to by a short fat man.

He picked up a glass and poured two fingers of whiskey from a crystal decanter. He held the glass to the firelight stared at the golden liquid for a moment and then tossed it back without the blinking of an eye. He turned back towards me, thought for a moment and then as if dismissing me walked across the room to a large leather-topped desk. He picked up a cheque book and flapped its pages in front of his face, waving it like a fan.

'I've written a figure here, Harper, it's twice as much as your place is worth on the current market. It's a very fair price and my advice to you is that you take it and ride on.'

I stared at him the anger boiling in my throat then cooling, stifling the words I wanted to say pushing them back for another time. I replaced my hat, walked back toward the still open door conscious of the thump of my boots on the polished boards.

'Well, Harper?'

I did not look at him, did not show him the bitterness I felt was apparent on my face. I stared out across the yard to where the old man was stroking the bay feeding it pony nuts.

'Your arrogance appals me, Belowen, but after looking at that picture it does not surprise me. You get your stock off Diamond H land or I'll get a county court order and confiscate them on account of fees owed for unpaid grazing rights. You put a rider on my land after you remove your beef and I'll run him off as a common thief. You send anyone against me and I'll send him back face down across his saddle. Good day, sir.'

I stepped out in to the fresh air and whistled the bay. It nudged the old man aside and loped over to me its stirrup fenders flapping. I swung aboard and thanked the man for his care. He grinned and nodded. Belowen stepped out on to the high porch and our eyes were on a level.

'You ought to think on it a while, Harper, things have changed since you were last out here.'

'I can see they have and not for the better.'

'Depends on your point of view. Most folk like things the way they are, the way I've made them.'

'Do most folks like the way the Diamond H was burned and an old woman killed and an old man crippled?'

'That what ires you, Harper, the old Nigger?'

He laughed and the coldness of his laughter followed me to the rise and even beyond that. I could still hear it when I was clear of Barking Dog range and riding my own boundary to where it crossed Blackwater Creek.

My encounter with Tom Belowen left me irritable and tired. Riding out there earlier that morning I had no real idea as to the kind of reception I might receive. A neighbourly welcome perhaps, a mis-understanding resolved, a rapid conclusion to our business, an agreement between two like-minded working cattlemen and a drink over a bargain struck. Instead I had found a threatening, bigoted man who, without ever meeting me face to face, considered me buyable even down to the number of dollars that would be acceptable to me. I wondered at his conceit and the strange emptiness of the place. I was still thinking of the man's cold, blue eyes when I cleared the ridge behind the line shack and saw the painted pony standing in the corral saddleless, head down chomping at fresh hay.

It took me nearly five minutes to make my way on foot down the slope keeping the cover of the trees between myself and the shack with the Winchester half-cocked and carried at the ready. Tangy grey smoke rose from the iron stack staining the clear sky and drifting off to the east. I had taken off my spurs and left them with the bay in the trees and cursed the squeak of my new left boot. Not really expecting any trouble this quickly I knew that I was being a little over-cautious but a man who took chances in a situation like the one brewing around me would have been a fool. And perhaps even a dead fool. I lifted the latch with the barrel of the carbine, pushed open the door and stepped into the gloom and as quickly to the right bringing the muzzle of the weapon to bear on Theresa Meyer's slim back.

I lowered the gun and grinned sheepishly as she

turned to face me. There were both moisture and laughter in her green eyes and her lips trembled slightly as she stepped towards me. I set the carbine on the table and without thinking reached out for her, pulled her to me, one hand around her waist the other holding the back of her head feeling the softness of her hair and pressing her face into my neck feeling the dampness of her tears and the warmth of her breath. I rocked to and fro with her and after what seemed forever she pulled away and reaching out for me pulled my face to hers and kissed me. Suddenly she turned, pushed her back into my chest and taking my hands she placed them on her breasts, held them there, pressed them to her and it was as if we had never left that line shack. As if we had stayed there the long years locked together in the pleasure and the nightmare of a dream broken now as the bay called down from the hill and the corralled pinto answered.

We lay together on the broad bunk, warmed by the heat of the open stove and by the thick Indian blankets my father had bought, for a long time after the sun had slipped beneath the western horizon flashing the sky with crimson and green before, finally, giving way to the silver starlit darkness of the clear night. Wrapped in our blankets we ate supper, drank coffee and sipped the whiskey I had packed in with the supplies purchased in Blackwater. We laughed a lot and cried a little as well, begrudging our lives the years we had spent apart and wondering how it could have happened. At such a moment of coming together it was easy to forget the pain of the circumstances that shape one's life and of the choices that have to be made. I supposed that would be something to reflect upon later when the immediate and burning passion of our renewed union was, through tiredness, quietened. Theresa told me only that Aaron Shiffner was an honourable man and would not marry a woman who did not love him. He helped her, supported her and Jonah and asked nothing in return other than her friendship, a commitment she was more than willing to give. Moke Calloway had told her the Shadow Rider would return, that he knew the President of the United States and his faith in that was unshakeable and she had believed the old Negro and waited with him.

At breakfast the next morning my left leg ached like it was going to fall off, a pain brought on I supposed, by the bitter cold of the night as I wandered naked, save for a blanket and my new boots, out to the cottonwoods to bring the bay down to the corral and feed it. The starlight bewitched me and, at the time, I felt nothing save the magic of the night and of the woman I had left sleeping in the line shack. Such foolish flights of fancy are for young men, I told myself, not for old gunfighters with bullet-shot legs.

Theresa sat opposite me nursing her tin mug and running her bare foot against my leg beneath the rough pine table. She had spent her time awaiting my arrival the previous day in cleaning and tidying up the shack and it was indeed comfortable and homely.

'Where had you been, yesterday I mean, before you tried to shoot me?' Her voice was soft, mocking but filled with a warmth you could touch.

'I rode out to Belowen's place, the Barking Dog, thought he should know how things were here now that I was back. Kind of let him know where the boundaries were and what I would accept from a neighbour, any neighbour.' I remembered again the man's cold, blue eyes and the harshness of his words.

'Tom Belowen is a strange man, Wes, better you be his friend than his enemy.'

Her eyes were worried, looking at me over the rim of the mug. Her foot was still.

'He's a mean man, Theresa, he tried to buy me out and when that did not work he threatened me. Veiled as they were in their lack of directness he left me in no doubt as to the meaning of his words.'

Theresa set down her cup and fetching the chipped enamel coffeepot from the hot stove she refilled both of our mugs.

'Be careful of him, Wes, he is a force around Blackwater.'

'You know him well? Did my father know him?'

She smiled at me at the mention of my father and I knew she was remembering him. A tall, handsome man with smiling eyes and a manner to match, the complete antithesis to Tom Belowen.

'Your dad died soon after Belowen arrived in the county but he did meet him on several occasions, said he did not care much for him. I don't know him well myself, his wife is friendly enough and his top hand, Art Coker, tries to spark me.' She cocked her head at me blew a kiss across the table and added, 'But that will have to stop now won't it, Wes, now that I have a real reason to discourage him.'

'I'll shoot his eyes out he so much as looks at you again.' I grinned at her, happier than I had been in more than five years and knowing why and not believing it to be really possible.

'On the face of it Belowen has done a lot for the town.' Theresa was suddenly serious again. 'He's raised the townspeople's hopes, brought in new merchants and businessmen, invested his own money in existing businesses, promised them the railway next spring. In all, on the face of it at least, Tom Belowen is Blackwater's future.'

'You see, hear any sign of the railroad coming this way? Surveyors, graders like that?'

'Not in town, although there have been surveyors working across and up from Laramie. They were at it for a month or so last summer stayed at the Barking Dog most of the time though. Why do you ask, Wes?'

There was concern in her eyes and although I did not want anything to cloud our hours together now that it was out in the open it seemed to me as good a time as any to deal with it.

'I've been away for a while what with one thing and another.' I shrugged, tried to smile the truth of the words away. 'But I know Wyoming, the railroad money and federal preferences where the West is concerned and I would have bet on Laramie, Orin or even Miles City in Montana as being the likely eastern railheads for drive-fattened beef, not way across here on the Powder. What do the other ranchers think?'

'There are no other independent ranchers, Wes, only you if you stay. The others have been bought out or swallowed by the Cattleman's Association of Blackwater Creek and Belowen is the Association.'

'You mean Belowen owns everything in the valley from the Big Horns through to Salt Creek?'

'I guess, accept for the Diamond H, he does.'

I creaked to my feet and stuffed some cordwood

through the open iron door of the stove, listening to it crackle watching the sparks leap from the burning sap as it oozed from the flayed bark of the logs.

Theresa smiled at me, walked over and put her arms around my neck. 'I told Jonah I would be away for a short time only; Aaron is a great uncle but a terrible mother. I have to get back this afternoon; you can ride in with me. Beside me.'

'Your old man?'

'He gave up on me years ago.'

'OK,' I agreed, 'but we have to stop off at the old Diamond H on the way, I need to think about that, rebuild it for you and Jonah. I take it you do want to stay around Blackwater?'

'Wherever you are or will be is where we will be, Wes.'

The words brought tears stinging to the backs of my eyes and I pulled her against me lest she see them knowing that she already had and that it did not matter in any way.

I took some rough measurements of the old house while Theresa patiently sat her pinto watching me as I picked my way through the fire-blackened ruin that had once been my father's home, was the killing ground of Florence Calloway and was my inheritance. In one corner of what had once been the main room I kicked at a pile of debris and a fire-blackened pocket-watch spilled from the ashes. I recalled my father standing there taking it out popping open the silver cover, consulting the enamel face and reckoning it was time for an evening drink. I slipped it into my pocket and continued my wandering. I made extensive notes with the stub of a pencil and then, together, we rode on, reaching Blackwater Creek by nightfall. The boy, a handsome ramrod-straight tow-haired, bright-eyed lad of twelve years was pleased to see me and Aaron Shiffner seemed unreservedly delighted at my return. I had supper with them and shaking hands with the attorney and rather formally with the youngster I stepped out on to Shiffner's porch. Theresa followed and we held each other close reluctant to be separated even for a short while. I told her I would call in the morning for coffee before returning to the line shack and that she and Jonah were welcome to join me any time either of them felt like it. For the first time in a long while I slept a deep relaxed sleep marred only once towards morning by the intrusion of Belowen's pale-blue eyes staring down at me from the portrait.

I was the first and I suspected only likely customer of the morning at the lumberyard. The proprietor a lean, bald-headed, pink-faced man with chewed-down fingernails and blunted, stumpy fingers stared at my neatly rewritten list and then back at me. His watery eyes dodging between the list and me like a snake faced with two fat mice and unsure which one to take.

'I can't do this, I'd sure like to but I just can't do it.'

He looked at me nervously and held the paper out for me. I didn't take it, left it there in his out-stretched hand.

'What's the matter with it?' I paused and read the name of the sign stretched across the front of the small office set in the centre of the yard. 'What's wrong with it, Heck?'

'Nothing's wrong with it, not a Goddamned thing.

It's a big order, bigger'n I've seen in a long while and I'd like to fill it for you but I just can't do it.'

'Why would that be, you've got it all in stock?'

'Mister Belowen, he passed the word down he don't want you accommodated in any way, passed that right down the line.'

'John Long shaved me this morning, talked with me, listened to me, took my quarter.'

Heck stared at me stony-faced.

'Belowen own the yard?' I asked, not letting the anger I felt boil to the surface.

'No he does not but he loaned me money to start out with and I, well, we all kinda owe him on it.'

I took a roll of bills out of my vest pocket and taking the note from him I wrapped it around the roll.

'That's more money than you will see in a long time, Heck, and who knows maybe it could even pay off your debt. One thing is for certain I will have that lumber, either from you or someone else. I send to Milltown they will freight it to me by wagon come the end of the month and charge me a little extra for it. I wait a week or so longer but I get it anyway and Milltown Lumber get the profit. Either that or you have the money now and I get the timber before the snow flies. Your decision but it seems a pity to let someone else take the money.'

Appealing to a businessman's common sense or to his better nature is not always an easy ride; on the other hand, appeal to a merchant's inherent greed and you cut a straight path to the action. Heck and myself parted on good terms shaking hands with the delivery of the lumber and tools promised for the following day. However, I made him give me a receipt just in case Belowen tried another tack.

\* \* \*

It was after dark when I crossed Blackwater Creek. The mud at the edge of the water had frozen hard in the first frost of the coming winter and the bay lost its footing on the ice, stumbling and shaking me to wakefulness. I cursed the cold creeping its way into my bones and steadied the animal watching our breath steaming on the night air. Our way was lit by the white silvery light of the stars and a half moon and the yard in front of the line shack sparkled with ice crystals. Maybe it was the cold, the aching leg or perhaps the all-round tiredness brought about by the unaccustomed activity since leaving Colorado's Cherry Creek or maybe it was a combination of all three plus the fact that I'm getting old, whatever, I failed to read the sign or smell the breeze and it cost me dearly.

They came out of the darkness at me in a rush. The bay reared as a moving figure slashed at its neck with a quirt and I barely had time to kick myself free of the stirrups and slide off before the frightened animal was galloping back towards the creek. I managed to land on my feet and clear the Colt, firing on the up as flame lashed out at me from the open doorway of the shack. I felt the burn of the passing bullet and busted a quick cap at the muzzle-flash, hearing a cry as another dark figure leapt at me a billy-club crashing down on my wrist, numbing it, jarring the pistol from my grip as strong arms wrapped themselves around my chest pinning my upper arms to my sides. I bent and twisted, flinging the cursing assailant over my shoulder and on to the hard ground. Before I could straighten another was upon me, then two, one holding me, bending me over backwards the other punching. I lashed out with a new boot jamming the high heel hard down upon a soft instep. The cry of pain pleasured me, as free, I rolled across the ground to where the pistol gleamed blue-black in the moonlight. I felt a sudden hard blow on my shoulder then heard the thundering report of a handgun, I felt no pain, not at that moment, that was to come later. The round knocked me forward and in seconds they were on me again, kicking and punching but no more gunfire. I held out as long as I could, not wanting to give way to the darkness that promised shelter and relief from the raining blows.

I could taste the dirt and blood in my mouth as I lay there no longer tormented by the shadows that had for so long pranced around me. I heard voices, one telling the others to leave me be, I had either got the message or I was a fool. I was in no position to judge which I was. The same voice telling someone to take my pistol and dump it then ordering another shadow to find the bay and kill it. Someone asked about firing the line shack and the voice laughed and said no, they would need it with winter upon them and no time to build another. Someone complained unhappily, a heavy accent, he was hurt and the voice telling him it was only a crease, to spit on it and shut his mouth. Then more laughter, banter from voices I would never forget. Then through the fog in my brain and the hissing in my ears the voices became clearer, unmistakable, the man giving the orders standing above me staring down I guessed, fixing my heaving back with pale-blue eyes. Then the words, 'You are one tough son-of-a-bitch, Harper, but to me you're nothing but white Nigger trash.' And the boot bouncing off my ribs.

And then they were gone, walking toward the woods where I guessed they had left their horses. I tried to rise but something popped in my shoulder and a wave of intense pain like a giant, black, thunderlit cloud washed over me and I gave myself to the night.

# TWELVE

I do believe in a Higher Power. There has to be more to the meaning of life than two weary legs walking the earth for such a brief span of time. My days with the US Marshals Service convinced me that beyond the ridge of our understanding, above the arroyos and the mesas of our desperation, there has to be a quiet force leading if not directing us along the path towards a better way. The evil thinking behind the destruction of the Plains Indian and the buffalo, the greed of the mining camps, the murderous inclinations of the border riff-raff and the desperadoes who kill without thought, the horror of the Civil War – all of these things and more have to be balanced by the good that is within the hearts of the majority of the people of this great country. The memory of a young man in Union blue and an old soldier in Confederate grey dying side by side upon the soft green turf of a Southern orchard surrounded by cornflowers and blackeyed daisies haunts me still and confirms within me the knowledge that the best is yet to come if the trail we choose to ride be an honourable one.

Twisting and turning on my bed of pain, trying

with great difficulty to distinguish a pleasurable horizon from the bad dream of the agony and discomfort racking the whole of my body, I questioned that Higher Power, faltered and then drew great strength from Theresa Meyer's soft answering voice. Her father ministered to my physical needs and she banished the doubt from within me with gentle words and promises of clear waters and sunlit days.

The men who came in the night and beat me near to death had not killed the bay pony. He was too quick for them. Bloody as he was from the blow of the quirt he had hightailed it back across country to Blackwater Creek and the stableboy who had shown him kindness. The deputy sheriff was not in town, being busily employed in the line shack's front yard, and the boy had alerted Aaron Shiffner who in turn had roused Doc Meyer and Theresa. They had found me in the morning lying halfway inside of the shack partially covered by a blanket I had seemingly dragged from the bunk, my life saved by the bitter cold of the night which had stemmed the flow of blood from my wounds and stilled any damaging movement.

I was bloody and most of my body bruised a yellowish purple. A pistol round had passed through my upper torso beneath the left shoulder-blade missing the bone and main arteries but tearing the muscle leaving the left arm stiff and sore. On the good side I still had all of my teeth, both my eyes – although one was darkly closed – my ears and, after a few days of nursing, most of my faculties. I also had a raging temper that flared up from moment to moment sometimes directed at my attackers and at other times against myself for

walking into the ambush. A lawman, even an
ex-lawman, of my years should have known better.

Theresa spent a great deal of time with me as did
Aaron Shiffner. The soft-spoken Doc Meyer
patched me up and expressed his pleasure at my
return, the past forgotten. I guess he was pleased
to see Theresa happy in my battered company.
Jonah visited for a spell and Moke Calloway moved
into the small outhouse next to the line shack. He
packed a sawn-off double-barrelled twelve gauge
shotgun which he bashed into about everything he
passed and the big Colt Dragoon's polished
wooden grips poked out of the deep pockets of his
army overcoat. He rarely spoke to me but watched
me when Theresa was away a sadness in his large,
watery, dark-brown eyes.

On the fifth day following the beating a
concerned-looking Aaron Shiffner visited with me
and Moke. Moke watched the tall man ride into the
yard, making certain he was a friend before
vanishing into the gloom of the outhouse to sit the
day away in the stuffed armchair he had had
packed out to the shack with him. No doubt he
watched the trail through a crack in the planked
wall. He had made the outhouse his domain and
any effort to entice him into the relative comfort of
the line shack had failed. I suspected Moke was
trying to make up for something he felt – quite
wrongly – responsible for. The only person or
persons needing to atone for the death of old
Florence that night were the gunman who pulled
the trigger and the man who had sent him there to
do it.

Shiffner pulled a chair up to the bunk and
offered me a cigar. I declined, my lips being

cracked and still swollen. I was fully dressed and sitting upright on the mattress, tired out and aching from my morning's regime of exercising. Most of me was now back in working order although there was still a certain stiffness in my left arm.

Shiffner was a little ill-at-ease and I wondered why. He stretched out his long legs beneath the bunk, hooked his thumbs in the vest of his dark suit and stared vacantly off somewhere in the middle distance.

'You find my Colt?' I asked.

'No, I checked the long grass and the creek as did Jonah but I guess it was stolen. Did find this though.'

He handed me my father's pocket-watch. It had been through the fire and now it looked as if it had been run over by a train. The front of the silver case was popped and hanging loose, the hands and the stem winder were missing and the white enamel face and glass cracked and broken.

'I guess that watch told its last time, Aaron.' I tossed the thing back to him. It was only a timepiece, the memory of my father was held hard and dear in my head and heart not in a chunk of scrap silver. He climbed to his feet awkward in my company for some reason I did not understand. I wondered if it was about Theresa but decided not and left him to work out his words whatever they might be.

'You ordered a bunch of tools and lumber from Heck Cole last week, told John Long you were set to rebuild the Diamond H I believe.'

'I made no secret of my intentions there. Has it been delivered yet?'

'No, and it won't be, at least, not by Heck it won't. Someone dragged him into an alley and worked him over almost as bad as they did you.'

'What sort of town you got here, Aaron? I've seen better behaviour in Wichita on a Saturday night.' I could not hide the anger in my voice.

'I thought we had a good town, a growing town, that is until you showed up again and now I'm not so sure.'

'It takes more than one man coming home to dirty the water.'

'I know it.' There was resignation in his voice as if he had thought it all through and was merely looking for someone to tell it to. 'Belowen has been good for Blackwater Creek. Invested his money where it counted, helped others, made promises we all want to believe. No trouble, at least none that we knew of. Last trouble of any kind we had around here was the killing of old Florence Calloway and that was just put down to drunken meanness getting out of hand. Then you show up and everything changes.'

'You like Belowen?' I said.

'He's not my kind of man, no, I don't like him but I have done a great deal of work for him. I handled most of his property transactions. He didn't buy from anyone who did not want to sell.'

'You certain of that?'

I saw the doubt in his eyes. Watched as he examined a detail here and a thought there. He shook his head turned his back on me and looked through the dirty glass of the window out to the empty corral.

'What do you make of him, Wes?'

Lying there on my bunk the last few days I had

given Tom Belowen a great deal of thought and believed I had the whole deal pegged. Not in any way because I was smarter than Shiffner or any of the other townspeople if it came to that, but because my whole life had been spent dealing with crooks and badmen. Outlaws come in all shapes and sizes and they don't all carry guns. Some creep up in the night and steal your boots because their own feet are bare but others come with money and a smile and while you're enjoying their company, they rob you blind of all that you hold dear including your pride and your dignity. In some ways, they are the worst kind of crook and often the hardest to catch.

I climbed stiffly off the bunk and took the last of Brubaker's Bull Durham from my freshly laundered shirt pocket and joined Shiffner at the window. Powdery snow like summer smoke was wafting about the yard twisting and turning in small waves at the every whim of the fresh westerly breeze sneaking into the valley from down and along the foothills of the Big Horns. Belowen was like that powder. One minute it was harmless and the next you were up to your neck in it and dying of cold.

'After the war carpetbaggers ravaged the South with their big ideas and their socks filled with Northern gold. They had little or no respect for the Southerners they went to fleece. I believe Belowen just reversed the trend is all. He came out West with a bucketful of money and he bought the soul of Blackwater Creek with the promise of wealth and a railroad. Well I don't think you are going to see that railroad, not for a good few years at least. If it does come it will go to Orin or Laramie and set there. In the meantime, the town will die or sell out cheap to Belowen at ten cents on the dollar and people will move on leaving a vast range and a town he doesn't really want or need to do with as he will. He is right about the cattle, the Texas herds and the great need for beef, but they will be his cattle not Blackwater Creek's.'

He turned to face me and even though his words denied me, I knew he saw the truth in what I had said.

'That simple? You really believe we were that gullible?'

'I know it, Aaron; the man bought your acquiescence with investment and good deeds. In real terms he has probably not ridden outside of the law in taking over the valley but look what happened the first time someone crossed him, he comes barrelling out of his hole with cannon blazing. Moke sitting on the only land he doesn't own and me in prison for twenty-five to life. I come back and Heck Cole steps out of line and you have two men down. That is a dark trail and who's next I wonder, and where's the law at? I'll tell you where the damned law is, it's sitting on its backside over at the county seat while the local deputy is out shooting at old Negroes.'

My voice had dropped to almost a whisper. There is never any denying your roots and for one brief moment there and then I would have packed Theresa and the kid in a wagon and headed south and east back to where the warm gulf wind blows off the saltwater and winter snow is the rarity rather than the rule.

'It's really not that clearcut is it, Wes?'

'No it isn't. You all got what you wanted at the time but the desire to grow got confused somewhere along the line with good old down-home greed and Belowen with his know-how and his dollar bills gave with one hand and took it all back with the other.'

Long after Aaron Shiffner had left for Blackwater I sat by the stove wondering why the hell I didn't just up and do it anyway, then old Moke came in for coffee and I remembered why.

Two days later Theresa brought the bay on a leading rein and leaving Moke Calloway installed and loaded for bear I rode back into Blackwater with her. Before leaving I had, under her curious gaze, lifted a floorboard and retrieved the silver Colt and its oiled leather holster from out of the recess. I cleaned and loaded the revolver and she noted the sentiment on its back strap and asked me about it. I said that one day I would tell her but not then. She smiled at me and kissed me and said she could wait.

The first light fall of snow had vanished only to be replaced the following day by a heavier fall and part of the trail was already buried in a two foot drift through which the bay and the paint cheerfully ploughed. My hands and feet were cold and my shoulder pained me some but I did not complain, happy to be out and doing something. We stabled our horses at the livery and I tipped the boy for his care of the bay. I kissed Theresa's warm lips delighting at the feel of her fresh cold nose and cheeks. She glowed with cold and her eyes shone like diamonds in red velvet. We agreed to meet for supper with Shiffner and the boy in the Cattleman's Hotel but I told her I had other business to take care of before the evening and I would call for her.

John Long shaved me but was not his usual talkative self. I doubt that he spoke more than seven words to me and two of those were hello and goodbye. I thanked him and walked across the deserted street to the Bluebird Café.

It too was empty that late in the afternoon and a bored looking Kelly Doohan walked over to take my order. Her eyes brightened a little when she recognized me.

'Heard you were back, Wes, thought maybe I recognized you when you first hit town, wasn't sure though who it was under all of that dirt.'

I stood up and touched her arm gently. The bruise was gone just a pale smudge of darkness remained.

'You're looking good, Kelly?'

'And you're a damned liar, Wes; still it does a girl good to hear a nice lie now and again. What can I get you, it's on the house.'

There was still a lovely smile on that tired face and a dangerous glint in her eyes I felt I should not notice or respond to. But it was hard.

'Coffee please, Kelly, hot and sweet.'

'You always did like it that way, Wes.'

She all but laughed aloud at my embarrassment as she turned back toward the counter swinging her hips and neat backside as she walked letting me know she wasn't tired all over.

I was half-way through my second cup of coffee enjoying the warmth of the place when the door opened and Chase Hawkins walked into the room bringing a flurry of snow with him. He froze in the doorway staring out from under his snow-speckled hat fixing me with his one good eye . His coat was open and I could see his star and that he was wearing a revolver on his right hip. I guessed the man to be a bully and I suspected that for one of the few times in his miserable life bravado overruled his innate sense of caution. He walked to my table and looked down at me touching the eye patch with his left hand as if to ensure it was still in place. There was snow on his moustache and I could smell the cold on him mixed in with the stale stink of tobacco that clings to a man when he smokes too many cheap cigars in an enclosed space.

'You don't listen good, do you Harper? I heard Mister Belowen told you to get out of Blackwater pronto.'

I rocked back on my chair cupping the hot coffee in my hands looking up into his dark, hard eye.

'You know something, Hawkins,' I said quietly, 'I don't mind much that you beat me half to death the other night or that you kicked me when I was down but I do resent the fact that you took a quirt to my pony.'

He was opening his mouth to speak, to maybe deny that which I knew to be true when I filled it and his eye with scalding hot coffee. He yelled and staggered away from me giving me room and time to get to my feet. I reached forward and jerked his sixgun from its holster and beat him around the head with the long steel barrel. Where his hands protected his face I beat them as well breaking two of his fingers and possibly his hand. I laid into him with a vengeance splitting his nose and ear, filling his eye with blood and finally chopping the piece down hard of the side of his head spilling his bulk on to the floor of the Bluebird Café. I emptied the pistol and dropped it and the brass shells beside him. Kelly Doohan moaned and I turned to face her reading in her eyes the terrible figure I must have appeared standing there over the fallen deputy. I tried to smile but it was a wasted effort so I wiped it away.

'When he comes to, tell him that was for Flo and Moke Calloway and tell him also, if he ever crosses my path again I'll kill him.' I dropped a quarter on the table picked up my hat and stepped over the groaning, bloody-faced Hawkins and out into the snow of the late afternoon, ashamed of myself and frightened by the anger that had possessed me.

Aaron Shiffner was late so we started without him. The hotel restaurant was empty save for ourselves and a pair of visiting southern cattlemen who were probably wishing they were still in West Texas. To Theresa's amusement the boy and I talked about spring colts and fishing holes. I promised him one of the former and he assured me that he knew the best and deepest trout pool in the county where cutthroats almost jumped into the skillet if the fat was hot enough. I wondered where he had learned such stuff and reckoned that Shiffner was a more sure-enough outdoorsman than he sometimes appeared. We ate our beef stew and were about to tackle a plate of sweet dumplings when the attorney arrived threading his way through the empty tables leaving a trail of snowflakes behind him. There was something about the man's mood. He was excited, triumphant almost. He sat down and pulled a piece of paper from his vest pocket, it was a telegraph form from the Wells Fargo office down the street.

'Sorry I'm late but I had to wait for this.' He held it up still folded. 'With the snow blowing in the way it is I figured the lines will be down pretty soon and this may be the last we hear of the outside world for a while.'

He was right of course. The winter played hell with the communications of the West. The stage would not be able to run and more often than not the linemen and their ever-moving train of wagons would not make it through the snow.

'What is it, Aaron,' Theresa said, her green eyes fixed on the waving paper.

Shiffner passed it to me and I opened it. The light was not good in the hotel's dining-room but the telegraph operator had a strong clear hand and the printed letters were not hard to read. It was from Washington, the office of the Chief Marshal of the US Marshals Service with a copy forwarded to the territorial governor in Cheyenne authorizing Shiffner to appoint me as a deputy for the Territory of Wyoming.

I passed it to Theresa who read it without comment and passed it back to Shiffner her eyes carefully avoiding mine.

'I called in a few favours from way back and it helped that a Marshal Brubaker has also shown an interest in your reinstatement as a deputy down in Colorado; however, that aside, someone heavy must have pulled a string to make it work this quickly.'

Shiffner stared at me as if waiting for something but I had nothing to give him. Not even my thanks. It was what I had wanted when I left Cherry Creek but that was before I had known that Theresa had waited for me. Now I was not so sure. There was a need for law in the county but after my behaviour with Chase Hawkins I was not certain that I was cut out for it any more. Shiffner seemed to read my thoughts.

'I contacted Mark Newell but he professed complete trust in Hawkins and more or less told me to go fly my kite.' He paused, reaching into his suit coat pocket. 'They couldn't send a badge down the wire but I had this fixed up for you.'

He handed me a small square of white linen at just about the same moment as his dinner arrived at the table. He didn't touch the food but watched as I unrolled the cloth. It was a silver badge made from the front plate of my father's pocket-watch. A highly polished wheel-badge with a star cut from its centre and the legend DEPUTY US MARSHAL stamped boldly around the outer circle. I did not know what to say or do at that moment. I looked from the attorney to the wide-eyed boy and finally to Theresa Meyer. I suppose I asked the question with my eyes and she answered it with hers and standing up she reached out for the badge, took it and walking round the table she pinned it to my vest and kissed me. I do not think I have ever been prouder in my whole life than I was at that moment. But the feeling was short lived.

Doc Meyer walked into the room, saw us and came over. There was anger in his eyes and blood on his hands and shirt cuffs. He glared at me as if all he had ever thought of me was suddenly confirmed.

'I've just finished sewing Chase Hawkins back together and now I suppose that Goddamned badge will give you the right to pistol-whip any man who doesn't agree with your way of doing things. Maybe you should never have come back to home, Wes, you're the worst kind of trouble there is.'

The old man had had his say; he glared at

Shiffner touched his hat to Theresa and gently patted Jonah's tow hair and then, turning from us, he walked back the way he had come.

It was not a heavy snowfall as Wyoming snowfalls go, just a feint, nature's way of warning us not to take her for granted and that more spectacular weather was to hand any time she wanted to deliver it. Still, it was enough to deter me from riding back to the Diamond H in the white darkness and I booked a room in the hotel taking a bottle of whiskey to bed with me wishing it were Theresa Meyer. I needed her warmth, needed to feel her close by me.

I explained to them about Chase Hawkins being there when Florence Calloway was killed and the ranch burned down and also that I had recognized his leaping at me from the darkness in the yard of the line shack. It helped but it did not make it right. Strangely enough I felt that Theresa had been the most sympathetic, understanding my anger and frustration that the law I held in such high esteem had once again let me down. She promised to talk to Jonah about it the following morning. Shiffner took a different view of the beating. I guess the burden of responsibility was with him. In part it had been his action that had given me back the badge and I suppose he was concerned that the authority that went with it might lead me into a course of action with which he wanted no part.

# THIRTEEN

Far off and to the north-east of Blackwater Creek up towards the old Bozeman Trail, on a tree-stripped meadow among the long grass and the summer wildflowers is the blackened, smoke stained ruin of Fort Phil Kearney. The Sioux under the leadership of Red Cloud burned it to the ground when the garrison departed in 1868 and it was the beginning of a peace of sorts. Now, out among the Dakotas there was once again the sound of white men on the move. Rumours of gold in the Black Hills and an army summer expedition to verify the fact had put the peace of the eastern side of Wyoming Territory on full alert with stories circulating daily that Sitting Bull – having succeeded Red Cloud – and Crazy Horse were preparing to defend the last of their homeland to the death. John Long had heard the stories and Nate Cooke carried news of them in the *Blackwater Creek Standard*. I did not for one moment doubt them to be true.

I was thinking of these things as I pushed the bay out along the snow-covered trail past the derelict Diamond H with its frozen watertank and frosty-backed round-eyed cattle. Belowen had

made no effort to draw his herd back across the
Barking Dog boundaries and the fact that there
were fewer cows on my property now than on my
last visit was purely down to the weather. The stock,
the smarter ones that is, were in the draws and the
sheltered gullies out of the snow, cropping at the
wind-cleared grass making the best of what
promised to be a bad winter.

Belowen aside, the badge carried far wider-
reaching responsibilities with it than the rights or
wrongs of a local carpetbagging. If the Indian
Wars did fire up again then the law in the federal
territories would have to be upheld by the Marshals
Service. I would not be alone out there and that
was a fact. Still it did complicate matters. My
accepting the badge meant that I could be called
away to any part of Wyoming at a moment's notice,
a thought that did not please me and one of which
Theresa Meyer was only too well aware.

Moke Calloway stepped awkwardly out of the
trees a hundred yards or so from the shack. His
eyes ran with the cold, his breath white and his bare
fingers looked as if they were frozen to the stock of
the scattergun. He limped over to me and taking
hold of a stirrup leather walked down the hill with
me to the cabin. I wondered where the crutches
were and guessed that, to a certain extent, they
were props for the old man in more ways than one.
There was smoke dribbling out of the stack and I
could smell it on the cold flat air. I tossed hay into
the corral and watched as the pony rolled in the
snow. I have never yet met a really smart horse.

I made coffee and breakfast for the both of us
during which the old black man never spoke a
single word to me. He grunted his appreciation,

nodded for coffee and sugar and grimaced at my flapjacks but he didn't speak, not until we were settled warm and comfortable in front of the stove's open door. Me with a ten-cent cigar and him with a chaw of tobacco I had brought back for him jammed up behind his gum, puffing his cheek, the black residual liquid tripping its way down a care line in his dark-skinned old chin finding its path like fresh water along a dry creekbed.

'Nobody came, Lieutenant, but they will. They came before and they'll come again you mark my words.'

The words sort of drifted out and I let them hang on the warm air drawing on my cigar and watching the ash glow and fade.

'Who would that be then, Moke?' I said, after a while.

'Hawkins, he'll lead them. Then the 'breed and the low-life from Blackwater. Not the Tollands though, they moved on when Mister Belowen bought 'em out. Monroe's boy drowned in the creek that year when it flooded and Sammy Ryan with him. Miss Kelly's daddy was drunk but Reno Taverno weren't and neither was the Mex, Santana Vallejo.'

I jammed fresh wood into the stove and tilted back my chair, pushing it back a little further from a blast of heat as the oily wood caught fire.

'I wish I'd been there for you, Moke.'

'You are this time, Lieutenant, and that will do.'

When I looked over at him again following a long silence I saw that he was asleep, his chest gently heaving beneath the tattered army overcoat he never seemed to be without.

During the next two weeks more snow fell and then

it all went, vanished, melted by a warm chinook wind that drifted across the flatland and through the valleys. It fooled the birds into nesting and wildflowers into sending their green spears out of the once again soft ground. It fooled me into starting work on the old ranch house. Clearing away the debris and burning it close to where I planned a flower and vegetable garden for Theresa, the wood ash enriching the soil. I worked alone, Moke would not leave the line shack convinced that as soon as our backs were turned it would be raided. I doubted that. Belowen's cattle were still around and I had no wish now to move them before the spring. Of the man himself I had heard little. On one of my several trips into town for supper with Theresa and an illicit but delightful night in a room of the Cattleman's Hotel, I heard that he had temporarily left the area to inspect his holdings on the eastern side of the valley out towards Salt Creek. John Long, friendlier this time, told me over a shave that a man named Reno George Taverno was looking after the Barking Dog and he didn't spit without first hearing Belowen clear his throat. I guess there was an indirect message of comfort there, something to tell me I was safe for a while at least. It amused me and angered me at one and the same time. I made peace with Theresa's father who told me he had treated a septic gunshot wound on the right arm of a half-breed named Santana who rode for the Barking Dog. He said that the man was reluctant to say how he had come by the wound but it did fit with my account about creasing one of my attackers, a man with a south-of-the-border accent.

The best news I gathered was from Aaron

Shiffner who reported that Hawkins had resigned and gone to work directly for Belowen and that a wire to Sheriff Newell at the county seat for a replacement met with the retort that, if Blackwater Creek had itself a resident US marshal it didn't really warrant spending county money on a replacement deputy sheriff. We both agreed that the absentee official was probably correct in his assumption.

The reward money, more than I had expected, for taking down Charlie Wilcox arrived from Brubaker only hours before the wire was cut far to the south of the Powder. Cooke reckoned it was probably the beginnings of fresh Indian problems as that was their usual first hit against the white man. 'Wells Fargo relay stations and the Goddamned telegraph wire.'

All in all those two weeks were a lot of fun. I took Jonah fishing and bought him the promised colt we would saddle-break and train in the spring. In the meantime the feisty animal was kept in one of the livery corrals and gave the boy the twice daily opportunity to visit with it and to talk to it of the great days to come when they would ride the open plains together with the Shadow Rider and his silver pistol. Theresa told me these things in the night and I smiled remembering my own childhood.

But the chinook passed and with it the warm days. The snow rolled in behind it killing the fresh green foliage and sending the birds back to their winter foraging, all thought of egg-laying forgotten. I gave up on the ranch and Moke and I settled in at the line-shack for a cold spell. I wondered if we wouldn't do better sitting it out in

town and I was thinking about just that when a
flurry of heavy calibre rifle slugs shattered the
window and the peace.

I guess it was no accident that the shooting
coincided with the rumoured return of Tom
Belowen a fact brought to us by an itinerant
cowhand looking for a hot supper and work. We
gave him the food, jawed a while and then sent him
on his luckless way. More than anything else
though, the shooting was an annoyance, in that it
kept the pair of us on our toes and short of sleep
waiting for the next attack. After two days of edgy
confinement with old Moke I said the hell with it
and saddling the bay and pinning my badge on the
front of my jacket where it could be clearly seen, I
rode out across the creek in the direction of the
Barking Dog. My thick canvas coat was buttoned
hard to the throat and I wrapped a scarf across my
forehead and knotted it behind my head in order
to stop my ears from freezing off. My hat, jammed
down hard, held it in place. I carried the Colt in the
jacket's deep right-hand pocket. A holster would
have been of little use if I needed the weapon
quickly.

It was a little after ten in the morning when I
rode into the Barking Dog's front yard. The sky
was grey and filled with meanness, the air cold and
the snow-spattered ground rock hard. Belowen
was standing on the porch an ankle-length
buffalo-skin coat draped across his wide shoulders.
A saddled pony was tied to the hitching rail, it's
hide and breath steaming as it snorted and pawed
at the ground. Belowen had watched me ride up
and continued to watch me his hands out of sight,
thrust deep into the long coat's pockets.

'Get down, Harper, and come inside, you look near froze to death.' His voice sounded affable enough and I stepped down. He took one hand out of a pocket and raised it high. A man with a rifle, the same old man I had encountered on my first visit, stepped out of a barn and walking over to us took both horses, leading them back to the shelter.

'Take good care of the man's horse, Art,' Belowen called after him.

'Art Coker?' I asked.

'Yes, why?'

'Oh, nothing,' I said, smiling to myself remembering Theresa's words and liking the fact that she teased me.

Thick logs were heaped and burning in the fireplace. A cowhand I did not recognize was sitting at the big desk. He stood up abruptly as soon as he saw me, scraping back the chair as I stepped into the room ahead of Belowen. He was tall, slim of build with long brown hair, a drooping moustache over a narrow mouth. Cold eyes flanked a hawk nose; my age or a year or two younger. The man's hand was reaching for his holstered sixgun but froze that way as Belowen walked into the room behind me.

'George, this is Harper; Harper this is my foreman Reno George Taverno, you may have heard of him,' Belowen said, shrugging out of the magnificent fur.

I nodded, stripped off my gloves, stamped some life back into my feet and undid the front of my coat. Just in case, I dropped my hand into my jacket pocket getting a firm grip of the pistol while I warmed my backside from the dancing flames. If they noted the fact that I was not wearing a sidearm they did not mention it.

'What can I do for you then, Harper? Drink?'

I shook my head and watched as he poured one for himself. He did not make the same offer to Taverno.

'Fancy badge, Harper, you intend to make use of it out here?'

'Maybe; someone took a shot at me the other night, broke a window and scared the hell out of me.'

'Hunter, maybe? All kinds of crazies out for deer when the winter really hits.'

'I doubt that.'

'Why are you telling me, Harper? You're the law, ride 'em down.'

'It was just a by-the-way, Belowen, I really dropped by to talk about your ramrod here.'

That got Taverno's attention.

'Oh yeah, and what would you be talking about me for, Harper.'

'Just asking you to stay in the county for a while, Taverno. I've got a signed deposition puts you out at the Diamond H the night Florence Calloway was killed and the place torched. Soon as the wires are singing again Cheyenne's sending me up a couple of warrants one for you and another for a half-breed Mex named Santana Vallejo. There's others of course and I'll get around to them all eventually.'

There was no such deposition of course and no chance at that time of Cheyenne sending any warrants, but Taverno didn't know that. He stepped around the desk his hand hovering above the wood grips of his holstered pistol. The movement startled Belowen who stepped toward him, hands raised in a calming motion. It did not stop Taverno and the man's hand dipped down to his holster. As his gun came up, Belowen, wide-eyed and obviously frightened by the turn of events, leapt to one side rolling clear, knocking over a heavy chair and cursing his man. With no time to withdraw the Colt I judged the angle and fired through the bottom of my jacket pocket.

The .45 round took Reno George Taverno in the chest about six inches below his narrow jaw; it staggered him backwards into the wall and his drawn pistol fell from his hand hitting the floor with a thud, the jolt discharging the weapon into the ceiling. The muzzle-flash of my own pistol set my jacket on fire and I pulled the gun clear and beat out the flames with my left hand.

Through the ringing in my ears I heard the raised voice of Belowen yelling at his wife to get out of the room. I turned in time to see the birdlike woman I had first met in Blackwater Creek vanish in a cloud of skirts.

'Jesus Christ, Harper, put up that Goddamned gun before someone else gets hurt.'

The cocked pistol was pointing directly at him; almost unconsciously I had covered my next expected target and had he made a wrong move I would undoubtedly have shot him as well. I lowered the hammer and keeping the weapon at the ready walked over to where Taverno was gasping for breath his eyes rolling upwards, dying even as I reached his side.

What happened next surprised me even more than Taverno had in trying to shoot it out with me in the ranch house of the Barking Dog.

Belowen pushed me to one side and knelt down by his dead foreman. He closed the man's eyes crossed himself and climbing awkwardly to his feet he turned to face me. I expected malice, anger, a tirade, accusations about trigger-happy lawmen but none of these things were said. He looked at me with his cold, blue eyes and touched my arm.

'I'll get you something for that hand, Harper. Mrs Belowen will fix it for you, it must hurt like hell.'

He brushed past me ushered out the three armed cowboys who had crowded into the room and were standing under my gun and called his wife. He poured and drank a large whiskey while the birdlike woman fussed over my scorched fingers with a salve that smelled like it might have been meant for horse doctoring rather than human ailments. But it was cooling and her touch was gentle.

Belowen looked over her shoulder at my hand and then at me, behind him the old cowboy and a younger man were carrying out the last earthly remains of Reno George Taverno who had drawn on an unarmed deputy marshal and bought himself some terminal grief.

'I had no idea George would make a play like that, Harper, I hope you believe me,' Belowen said.

'You did look kind of surprised.' I kept my voice cool and official, the badge talking, not sure where the man was coming from.

He handed me a shot-glass and I tossed the drink back, needing it.

He refilled his own larger glass and stared into it and then over to me, as his wife, muttering under her breath, finished her doctoring, picked up the jar and remainder of the bandage and crossed the room settling quietly on a corner chair her birdlike and anxious eyes fixed on her husband.

'I'd also ask you to believe I had nothing to do with

the killing of the old Negro woman either or burning down your daddy's place. Don't get me wrong, I don't hold with blacks being better off that white men and it's on account of them the South died, but I don't hold with killing old folk either. People, headstrong and foolish people, out to please me I guess.'

'And Heck Cole? And out at the line camp? You were just passing by there and stopped for a glass of lemonade I suppose?' The sarcasm was not lost on him.

'That was personal, Harper, you come by here and threaten me in front of my men and I have to do something about it. I was angry, not thinking clearly. It happens.'

I thought of the shock on Chase Hawkins's face when I laid into him with the pistol barrel and silently agreed with Belowen.

'Heck Cole? Poor bastard; people out to please me again, Harper. Thing is it may well have been one of my hands took a shot at you but not under my orders. Chase Hawkins will kill you for sure if he gets the chance and he's no mean man with an iron but him and the 'breed you are looking for are camped out over at Salt Creek keeping an eye on the Dog's eastern boundary. It's going to be a long winter for the pair of them, but I'll put the word out anyway that it wouldn't pleasure me to have you taken down, not because of the badge, I don't give a shit about Yankee law, but because it doesn't matter that much to me. I've got the valley sewn up tight and I own most of the town. I don't need the Diamond H. Not one square foot of it.'

'And what are you going to do with the valley now you have it?'

'Hold on to it, wait for the war. It'll come soon

enough, probably already started out in the Dakotas. The army will move in in force and buy beef for themselves and then for the Indians when they corral them. The miners who'll rape the hills will need feeding and, the best of it is, the beef walks right up to their dining-table and I don't need any Goddamned railroad.'

'The town does.'

'Then maybe, God willing, one day they will get it but most of them won't stay around long enough to see it.'

'A ghost town is all you'll have.'

'A ghost town is all I need.'

'You really are something, Belowen.'

'I've done nothing more than the Northerners did and are still doing to the South. You wouldn't recognize parts of Texas, take my word for it.'

I gingerly slipped a glove over my left hand and picked up the Colt, shoving it into my pants waistband just behind the belt buckle.

'That's a fancy piece, Harper, couldn't help noticing the sentiment. Whose life you save could afford a gun like that?'

I couldn't help it and I knew I should not but in truth it would mean little to him and a great deal to me. 'The man who gave me that Colt whipped yours and old Bobby Lee's asses all over, Belowen, from Washington through the Shenandoah Valley and clear to the Savannah Sea.'

I left him thinking about that, touched my hat to the woman and stepped aboard the saddled bay. I kneed the animal out of the Barking Dog yard, feeling tainted by the man who was counting on another suffering-filled war to make him an even richer man than he already was.

# FOURTEEN

Something went out of me that afternoon at the Barking Dog and when I awoke the following morning after a restless, fretful night filled with the echoing sound of Reno George Taverno's death rattle, I had made up my mind, if Theresa agreed, to let the Diamond H go. Over breakfast I managed to get through to Moke Calloway that Taverno was dead, that the line shack would be safe and that it was time for us to be moving on.

'As soon as we's gone they'll be coming by, Lieutenant.'

'No, not any more, Moke, it's over.'

'Not with Chase Hawkins it's not; I shot his eye out with a piece of wood and he promised one day he'd kill me cold.'

'He's gone and when he comes back I'll arrest him for what he did to Florence. You rest easy, old friend.'

'He meant it for sure.'

We could have gone on arguing about it all night, in some ways he was like a child demanding the last word but, I suspected that deep down he was probably correct in his assumption that Hawkins would come back. Shiffner had told me that the old man had lived under his and Doc Meyer's protection from the day of the burning but Hawkins had often cast his mean eye in the old Negro's direction.

With Shiffner's help I rented a small house off Main Street not too far from where the Meyers lived making it easy in the bad weather for the boy, Theresa and myself to drift from house to house and to get used to the permanence of each other's company. There was a small annexe to the house and after a great deal of coaxing, much of it generated by Theresa, we persuaded Moke Calloway to move out of the boarding-house and set up home with me. Although he trusted my judgement and my assurance that we were not in harm's way his gnarled old hand was never far from the big Dragoon Colt.

Theresa and I talked about the Diamond H and when we had all but talked it to death we asked Jonah to join us. I proposed letting Aaron Shiffner get the best price he could for the property from Belowen whom I suspected, in spite of his exhortations to the contrary, would like to round off his boundaries and complete his takeover of the valley. I further proposed that with part of the money we should outfit a wagon and, come the spring, head south and east to Texas with maybe a stopover in Denver to get married and to honeymoon there while Brubaker took the boy off to the Cherry Creek cabin for a fishing holiday.

While the boy's enthusiasm for Texas seemed to know no bounds, Theresa was a little more reserved. I understood her worries; it was a long way from her home, her father and friends. I suggested that there was as much a need for doctors in Texas as ever there was in Wyoming and if he was of a mind to he could join us later, the Union Pacific running clear from Cheyenne to Fort Worth. She agreed to talk to her father about it but insisted that whatever he said would not influence her decision. I had made it clear to both her and the boy from the very beginning that it was only a proposal and if they preferred to stay in Wyoming then that was where we would stay. However, in my heart of hearts I hoped they would choose the adventure. And so they did.

I could almost feel the warm gulf wind on my neck and see the two of them sun-darkened and fresh-faced watching the seabirds at sunset tasting the salt-tanged air as it breezed its way in across the blue waters. It was accepted that where we went then so too would the old Negro and although I never talked to him about it directly he knew that his future lay with the three of us and he was not displeased with that fact.

There was very little real need for the services of a US marshal in Blackwater Creek following the short-lived feud with Belowen and although I did spend some time on official duties as requested either by the mayor or, when the telegragh was working, in response to directives from Cheyenne, most of my time was spent poring over maps, checking on the wagon we had bought and digging through my recollections of trails ridden many long years before.

Christmas came and went and, towards the end of January, I received a wire from Brubaker the contents of which disturbed me considerably.

Brubaker reported that George Benteen had beaten a shackled prisoner to death in a county

jailhouse and had fled the scene only hours ahead
of a warrant for his arrest. A US deputy had trailed
the fugitive almost to the New Mexico border and
lost his man in the badlands south of Trinidad. A
later report from the Kiowa County sheriffs backed
by a sighting in Yuma County suggested the
fugitive could be circling east and north with
Wyoming a possible destination. Brubaker stressed
these were unconfirmed reports but knowing the
hate in the man for me, he counselled vigilance. I
talked it over with Shiffner and we both agreed
that Benteen would be a fool to head north at that
time of the year and an even bigger one to go
against a deputy US marshal. I thought about that
late into the cold night over a drink of hot coffee
laced with whiskey and knew that Brubaker had
been right to warn me.

'You really think this man Benteen would come
up here to kill you?' Theresa snuggled against me
listening to the almost unbelievable silence of
falling snow. It banked and muffled every night
noise in Blackwater and insulated the senses as well
as the buildings against any outside intrusion.

'Brubaker thinks he might so I guess it is possible
but it's something to be aware of not to worry
about.' I kissed the top of her head smelling the
natural perfume of her freshly washed hair.

'If it isn't Benteen then, it would be someone
else?'

I sensed the beginning of a storm and tried to
ride out of it by changing the subject, talking about
the boy's colt and how we would trail it and the bay
behind the wagon. Theresa stayed with her storm.

'What will you do in Texas when you are tired of
cows?'

We had never actually talked about that side of our new life together and I guess it was a natural enough assumption on her part that we get a homestead or something somewhere along the way. I shifted uneasily and she was on to it like a shot, pushing away from me, rolling to one side, her naked shoulder clear of the blanket, her green eyes shadowed in the light of the turned-down lamp.

'Why haven't we talked about this part of it before, Wes?'

I did not answer.

'Your father told me once that you would always be behind one badge or another. What will it be in Texas? A ranger? A sheriff? A transfer from Cheyenne to Dallas with the service?'

There was anger in her voice, a frustration of sorts and I was at a loss as to how to best deal with it. Her back was to me and I kissed her neck and shoulder but she didn't respond and after a while I assumed she was asleep and I settled on my back drifting off into a land of fiery, silver shields, sheriff's stars and Texas Ranger badges forged from five peso pieces. When I awoke in the morning as tired as when we had gone to bed, Theresa was not beside me. She did not come to me again until the evening and then she came with tears in her eyes, hot wet lips and the promise that whatever happened, whatever we did we would do together and never be separated. The next day she moved into the house with Jonah and in spite of the wagging tongues we decided to leave our marriage in abeyance until we reached Colorado.

One dark-grey, early morning towards the end of March we awoke to the sound of a constant dripping. Running water twisted its sleek way down glistening stalactites the drips getting bigger and the ice spears thinner. Water ran from the gutters and occasionally there was the swishing sound of snow sliding from pitched roofs and into alleyways along Main and Belowen Streets. The thaw had arrived early. Later in the day to our great delight the flat leaden sky cracked in the middle and around the ragged edge of the widening wedge-shaped hole the clouds glistened with burnished gold and the sun, hidden from us for so long, sent great shafts of sunlight down upon Blackwater Creek. Although the snow was still thick and drifted in the draws of the higher ground and the peaks of the Big Horns still flashed white against the last of the winter sky, it quickly vanished from the open flatlands below.

Main Street was a quagmire with water-filled ruts which froze in the still cold nights and melted into a thick reddish brown soup by every midday. The ruts were in part deepened by the heavy wagons leaving Blackwater Creek, filled with the belongings and families of one business or another as the realization that the railroad was not an immediate future prospect sent the merchants who had waited so full of hope for the boom, packed up and headed south before the expected Indian War erupted into a bloody reality. The wire had been down since before Thanksgiving but rumour, like the wind, had constantly invaded the privacy of the town houses with weary words of a broken peace as Custer's Seventh Cavalry expedition into the Black Hills of Dakota had confirmed the presence of gold.

I had promised Belowen a ghost town and it

looked like I was to be proven right. Heck Cole was
the first to leave, his lumber wagon packed with his
furniture and trappings. He had refunded the
money on my timber order and I, in turn, had
given him a percentage of the fee for the trouble
and pain he had attracted to himself on my behalf.
I waved at him as he passed the town hall and he
grinned back. Others quickly followed; John Long
packed his new barber chair and his wash tubs and
headed for the Dakotas along with Nathan Cooke.
Bob Brown packed as much of his beer hall stock
with him as he could selling the rest off at a bargain
price to Harmon David who decided to stay on for
a while saying he started out with a spit and
sawdust saloon and was happy to go back to doing
just that.

I spoke with Wall-eyed Wally Doohan who tried
through an alcoholic stupor to grasp what I was
telling him. He was the last of the mob who had
attacked the Diamond H still living in the county.
But I really wanted it over with and Kelly told me
she was packing the pair of them off to the East
and they probably would not stop until they
reached the ocean.

'I'm glad you came back, Wes.'

She must have read the disbelief on my face.

'Sure you ended the dream here in Blackwater
but it had to end sooner or later and maybe I do
still have a few good years left in me. I have
managed to save some money and Tom Belowen
waived the loan on the Bluebird.'

That didn't really surprise me at all, the man had
all that he wanted and more.

I took my hat off to her and kissed her lightly on
the cheek. 'I meant what I said about you looking

good, Kelly, and city life will suit you just fine. Keep that old man out of trouble.'

She touched my hand and was gone.

Theresa and I decided to await the real spring not wanting to subject ourselves or Moke and the boy to the bitter cold of sleeping out in the open on what was after all, still a winter's trail.

I met Belowen face to face only one more time and that was in Shiffner's quiet little office where I signed away the Diamond H for the same sum he had first offered me for it. We shook hands on the deal and the smile on his face was not one of gloating. I actually believed he was sorry to see us go. Other matters were also resolved during those few weeks leading up to the end of April and the beginning of May. Doc Meyer decided to join us in Texas and Shiffner said that he would accompany the old man on the long train journey and, if neither of us objected, he would like to join us in our new life. I could see that Theresa was pleased with the prospect probably hoping, quite correctly, that the attorney's influence on Jonah was a good one offering the boy many of the things I could not.

One Sunday two days before our scheduled departure following a near empty church service I kissed Theresa and swung aboard the spring-salty bay with a gunnysack containing a cold chisel and a hammer resting across my lap, I headed out toward the ruin of my father's ranch. I intended to chip out the keystone of the fireplace of the old chimney and reuse it in the fireplace I hoped to build for us in Texas.

The trail along the creek was dry, cracking in places from the constant gaze of the spring

sunshine. The creek itself was still in flood swollen
to three times its normal width and depth by the
melting snow running off and down from the
faraway mountains. Trout sparkled in the clear
water, hiding in deep sheltered pools away from
the main swish of the fast-moving current. Flat
sections of the ground were flooded an oily brown
where the creek had burst its banks and the damp
water-filled meadows had themselves been
churned up by the moving hooves of Barking Dog
cattle. A pair of red-tailed hawks were working the
margins and as I rode splashing through the water,
a newly arrived flight of duck took to the wing in a
rag-bag of a cackling formation. Before he had quit
Blackwater the gunsmith had sold me an English
12 gauge with a scrolled breech-block and a
beautifully figured walnut stock. I promised those
noisy duck that I would come calling before we left
or maybe meet them on the trail a little further on
down the line. I was feeling good, cocky and
pleased with myself, the nightmare of the previous
year almost forgotten. Indian Springs and the
Colorado Territorial Prison, Lattimer, Wilcox and
Taverno, places and people, things to disturb my
nights on and off forever but never to the extent
where I would not find relief in wakefulness, in
Theresa Meyer's arms or the blush of a Western
sunset.

My mind buzzing as it was with thoughts of the
life and the long trail ahead I failed to scout the
ruin of the Diamond H before dismounting and
setting about my chore with hammer and chisel.
Had I been more aware I would have seen the
freshly made tracks of two shod horses and known
that I had unwelcome and unwanted company.

# FIFTEEN

I sat on the fence rail of the old corral and bit the end off the last of Long's five-cent cigars. It was a warm sunny afternoon. I lit the smoke with a blue-top match and stared across at the blackened stone chimney rearing out above the ash and towering over the remaining scorched timbers of the ranch-house floor. I pictured my father standing there warming his backside. I could almost hear again the crackle of the ponderosa pine logs as I would listen to him bemoaning the fact that it was never warm in Wyoming, not even in summertime, as it was in South Texas. I looked above the stack to where a skein of mallard were circling the cottonwoods, making their landing approach to the waterlogged meadow beyond the trees. Suddenly they balked, swerved away from the cover and arrowed off low and fast across the grassland. The hairs of my neck bristled and I threw myself from the rail cursing my negligence. As I hit the ground on all fours wood splintered from the rail and my hat was torn from my head, the bullets rapidly followed by two echoing rifle shots. I danced and dodged my way across the yard to the shelter of the chimney drawing the Colt, angry at having left the bay tethered to the windmill, both it and the booted Winchester carbine beyond my reach.

With my back pressed against the stonework I peeled off the work gloves and flipping open the loading gate of the Colt I half-cocked the piece and rotated the cylinder to the empty chamber I always carried under the hammer. I dropped in a shining brass .45 round and closed and holstered the gun. Getting to my knees I tried to peer around the structure looking up toward the woods. Chips of rock flew from the stonework above my head and lead rounds screamed off into the brush behind me. I ducked back and within seconds two more shots coming in from below me thudded into the charred timber. A crossfire, I had to get away from there. I bellied down and squirmed across the charred boards rolling clear at the end and then underneath the remains of the porch. I waited listening.

'How you doing in there, Marshal? I'll smoke you out come nightfall like I did the old Nigger.'

Laughter, then more laughter from the trees and another flurry of shots ricocheting off the chimney. They hadn't seen me move and I had them roughly positioned for all the good it was likely to do me. Hawkins, for it was his voice that had called up to me, was somewhere out back of me by the creek below the windmill shooting uphill. The other gun was in the cottonwoods behind the chimney, the half-breed, Santana Vallejo perhaps.

I did not want to lie there until nightfall; sooner or later one of them would get around to shooting the fidgeting bay in case I tried to make a try for it.

On the other hand I wasn't exactly in much of a position to make their lives as difficult as they were making mine for me. But there was something I could maybe do, it called for timing and a lot of luck but I had seen it done once before. Out in the badlands to the north of Fort Worth, a Texas Ranger pinned down in some scrub by a bunch of Kiowa bucks and beyond the reach of my handgun. He had made it back close enough to my position for covering fire and escape. He called it the 'possum' roll and that had been how he was called from that day on. If Possum had made it then so perhaps, could I. Rolling out from the shelter of the boards I leapt to my feet ran four yards counting the steps then I twisted, jerked and fell at exactly the same pre-judged moment as one of the rifles opened up on me. I had hoped it would be Hawkins, shooting up hill at a moving target is one hell of a trick. It was, and the rounds reached out for me, brushed me with their passing as they buzzed close to my ear but they did not touch me. Out of the gunmen's view I slithered like some Goddamned sidewinder to the partial shelter of the corral watertrough and lay there motionless the Colt cocked and ready in my hand.

'I got him, I think I got the son-of-a-bitch. Right through the pump, he went down hard. Can you see him?'

I did not dare breathe through the following long silence.

'Maybe you did, Chase, and then again maybe you didn't. I can't see him from here and he's a tough old bastard.' Vallejo the half-breed from behind the chimney.

'I got him clean I tell you, go check him out.'

'You go check him out, you shot him.'

'Don't you shit me, Santana, go see to it.'

'Not today, Chase, this ain't Barking Dog time.'

'Damn you, keep me covered.'

'Gotcha, Chase.'

I rolled over on to my stomach; I could hear movement below me and away to the left but I could see nothing. I crawled away from the trough reasoning that if I could not see them then they could not see me. I made fifteen, twenty yards around the length of the ruin coming out of the dust and into the long grass by the nearest cottonwood. With my back against the tree and with it between me and the noisy Hawkins I slowly straightened. As my head came above the brush I came face to face with the startled half-breed. Vallejo twisted the Winchester towards me firing from the hip. The first round thudded into the tree by my left ear and I fanned three quick rounds into his chest which was three-quarters on toward me. The heavy bullets turned him away sending his next shot wild and high as my third round took him in the back pitching him on to his face. He did not utter a single sound from start to finish. I waited for the echo to die then dropped back to my knees, ears hissing, the powdersmoke of the Colt's discharge causing my eyes to water.

'Vallejo, Vallejo, what the hell's going down?' Hawkins, from close by, his voice almost a whisper.

'The 'breed doesn't hear so well anymore, Chase.'

My softly spoken words were answered by a fusillade of carbine fire tearing at the bark of the cottonwood sending green splinters raining down upon my head. I stood up and snapped off a quick round drilling it through Hawkins's tan hat, whisking it away and into the brush. He ducked down and out of sight and at least I had the satisfaction of knowing we were even in the hat department. I reloaded the empty chambers of the Colt and guessed Hawkins would be doing the same thing with his saddlegun. For the next fifteen or twenty minutes we took quick and unaimed shots in each other's general directions both of us, I supposed, hoping for a lucky hit. After a while Hawkins called out to me; he sounded tired.

'Harper, we could hide here 'til dark and gone taking pot shots at each other and burning up a lot of powder for nothing.'

'You have a better idea, Hawkins?'

'Yeah, out in the open, man to man with pistols, fastest gun wins.'

'You would lose, Hawkins, the hard way.'

'I'll take my chances against you, old man.'

Suddenly my age was an important factor. Vallejo had called me a tough old bastard. I didn't much care for it. 'You got it, Hawkins, only I don't trust you a whole lot. Toss out that carbine and you step out with your piece holstered and your empty hands out to your sides and we'll do it, otherwise no deal.'

'How do I know I can trust you?'

'You don't, that's the pleasure of it.'

A long painful silence and then, 'OK, Harper, I'm stepping out in the open.'

Hawkins's great bulk arose up from the brush, he tossed the carbine to one side and stepped out into a clearing maybe fifty, fifty-five yards away from me. A fair distance for the pistols.

Even with the passing of the months my mark

was still upon him. Angry white scars ran the length of his face from the edge of his short-cropped hair beneath his eye patch and down to his red-jowled chin, here and there crossing older, greyer ones. His hooked nose was bent and his left cheek-bone misshapen. Hate burned in his black eye and I could not blame him for that. I started to walk towards him figuring he would let me get as close as he dared. But he didn't wait. As soon as I moved he drew and fired three badly aimed rounds. Two pulled off to my right and one clipped the brush near to my feet. I crouched, drew, straight-armed the Colt and fired all six at him. The first was off to the left the second clipped his neck but the remaining four grouped in around his throat and upper chest. He sat down hard and dropped the gun, choking, grabbing his neck, pulling at his shirt collar his open mouth spilling blood down his chin. Then he rolled over onto his side as if sleeping and did not move again not then, not ever.

I walked over to where he lay, glad that it was done. I kicked his fallen revolver away from his outstretched hand and made my weary way down to the ruins to where a heavily bearded George Benteen was standing by the chimney, leaning against it, waiting, a Winchester in his hands the muzzle pointing directly at my breast. The Colt was still in my hand I brought it up and he grinned a broken-toothed grin as the hammer dropped on an empty shell casing.

'Careless of you, Harper, you capped all six at that sorry son-of-a-bitch.'

I started to move, tensed my leg muscles and he read the movement.

'Twitch and you're dead where you stand, Harper; I'm in no real hurry to kill you, it's been a long ride and a long winter but I won't hesitate if you make one move I don't tell you to make.'

'Go to hell, Benteen.'

'You first, jailbird, but you won't be taking that pretty pistol with you.'

He took several paces towards me the muzzle of the carbine never faltering. I thought of Theresa and the boy and of the packed and waiting wagon, of Texas and the warm Gulf winds. I thought of my father and mother and old Moke Calloway. I had no doubt whatsoever that George Benteen was about to kill me either standing or running, away from him or at him, it would make little difference in the end. And as I was trying to think my way through my life and death he stepped jerkily forward with an expression of utter disbelief on his florid face as his shirtfront pocket and Bull Durham tobacco sack exploded and a rifle crack he never heard whipped down at us from the cottonwoods behind the house.

I stood there like a scarecrow, hatless, my vest and Levis dusty and dirty from rolling about in the yard and the woods, rooted to the spot. I raised my eyes from where Benteen had fallen and looked off toward the trees to where a tall figure emerged from the late afternoon shadows and walked in my direction. He wore a high-crowned black hat and a long dun-coloured duster. He carried a Winchester rifle at the trail and walked quickly and easily down through the brush and the trees to stand in front of me a wide smile on his sad, handsome face. He stuck out his hand and I took it in mine.

'How many more times I got to keep this bastard from taking you down, Wes?'

I looked down at Benteen and with the toe of my boot I rolled him over on to his back. Blood was pumping from a great hole in his chest three inches to the left of centre, its flow a mixture of dry tobacco and red dust. His eyes were rolled up into this head and I knew that he had no idea as to who or what had killed him and in some perverse way that pleased me a great deal.

'Not ever again, Jack, you done him in for sure this time.' I slipped the empty Colt back into its holster not bothering to reload it.

'I've been following him hard for three days now. Picked up his trail in Fort Laramie, on a tip-off from a sheriff's deputy. We tried to telegraph you but the wire's still down and I guess it will be staying down for some time to come if Sitting Bull and Crazy Horse have their sweet ways.'

'It's started then?'

'All but the shooting. We far from Blackwater Creek?'

'An hour maybe.'

'You want to pack them in or bury them out here?'

'I don't feel like digging holes today.'

'Me neither, I'll catch up their ponies. Them other two, they friends of yours?'

He was still grinning and as my heart quietened down and my breathing eased some of the tightness out of my chest I realized how pleased I was to see him and of the things we had to talk about. And then of showing off Theresa and the boy to him.

'It's a long story, Jack, but they are both implicated in a murder that took place some while back.'

'And where was that?'

'I would say just right about where you are now standing.'

He looked down at the charred and splintered boards and then walked off to where a horse whinnied in answer to the frightened bay.

# Epilogue

I halted the team on the last ridge from which Blackwater Creek was visible. The running water sparkled and was once again imprisoned by its wide banks. Smoke drifted up from the iron chimneys of several of the town's still occupied buildings. Two heavily laden wagons cut east from along Belowen Street, their occupants heading towards the goldfields of the Dakotas hoping for a bucket of nuggets before the fall would drive them back to the townships that would be springing up along Beaver Creek, the Belle Fourche and the Cheyenne Rivers. The Sioux and the Northern Cheyenne would fight hard and maybe score a point or two but in the end dark-suited men in Washington who had never themselves ventured west of the Ohio River would sign the Indian lands away and send an ever increasing number of troops to ensure that their will be done. I was not sorry to be leaving it all behind us.

It had been a little over six months since my release from Colorado's Territorial Prison and in that time I had found Theresa and the boy, destroyed the hopes of a growing township and killed five men. Three of them were buried in the small cemetery at Blackwater Creek and although, from that ridge I could not make out their individual markers, I knew and would always know that they were there, part of me and yet not part of me. Memories to carry along whatever trails I might ride for as long as I lived. Desperadoes whose train had finally arrived. I felt a sadness for them that they did not deserve and felt a heavy burning at the back of my eyes.

Brubaker agreed to ride the point as far as Cheyenne but there he would entrain for Denver and meet with us again at Cherry Creek where he promised he would take care of Jonah for a week while Theresa and I had us a high time. The boy sat looking out over the wagon's tailgate with old Moke beside him the both of them watching our back-trail and the bay and the colt we had tied there.

'You never did tell me where you got that fancy pistol, Wes,' Theresa said as we rolled down the far side of the ridge.

'I didn't?'

'You don't have to tell me if it means breaking a confidence.'

'It would be OK to tell you, Theresa.'

'But you really don't have to if you believe it wrong to tell me.'

'I want to tell you.'

'Tell me then.' She pressed her body against me and held her flushed cheek to my shoulder.

'It was back in Maryland after the war on a sunny day that began much as today did.'

And then I told her the story of how I had earned that fancy revolver. She listened quietly and Brubaker waved as he cantered his big sorrel through the sweet-smelling prairie grass and the long Texas trail stretched out before us.